McCraw

AR: 6.0

BEORN THE PROUD

Beorn
the
Proud

by
Madeleine Polland

Illustrated by
Joan Coppa Drennen

BETHLEHEM BOOKS · IGNATIUS PRESS
BATHGATE, N.D.   SAN FRANCISCO

© 1961 Madeleine Polland

Cover illustration © 1999 Gino d'Achille
Cover design by Davin Carlson

Interior artwork © 1999 Joan Coppa Drennen

All rights reserved

First Bethlehem Books edition, October 1999

ISBN 978–1–883937–08–9
LCCN: 98–73485

Bethlehem Books • Ignatius Press
10194 Garfield Street South
Bathgate, ND 58216
1-800-757-6831
www.bethlehembooks.com

Printed in the United States on acid free paper

Manufactured by Thomson-Shore, Dexter, MI (USA); RMA587LS200, December, 2012

For the Black Strangers of Kolinggade

BEORN THE PROUD

CHAPTER ONE

THE SUDDEN BREEZE before the dawn stirred the rushes round the island, rocking the small boat which lay among them. In the bottom of the boat a girl moved and woke, confused first at where she found herself. Then she remembered clearly and all the happenings of the previous day came back to her as in a dream of terror. She lay still, looking backwards to the moment yesterday when she had crept happily among these same rushes on the other side of the island. Thigh-deep in water, she had searched for the nests of wildfowl, to surprise her mother with the brown, strong-flavoured eggs which she so valued for the table.

The monastery bell had startled her, clanging violently in the quiet air, but she was not yet frightened—perhaps it was a fire among the island huts or a pack of wolves marauding from the forest by the abbey on the lake shore. Idly, she had parted the tall rushes and peered out between them, only to see great white and scarlet sails spaced all across the lower lake, billowing above long-boats which bore

1

down upon the islands in speed and silence, like huge and brilliant birds of death.

She had not been able to get back to the village in the centre of the island. She had splashed and clawed her way in panic to shallower water, only to realize that the mighty ships were closing even faster than she upon the shore. There had been nothing left to do but hide among the rushes and watch in helplessness as the dark invaders swarmed from their beached ships and poured yelling up the shore to fall upon her father's village.

Now she could no longer bear her thoughts and sat up abruptly in the boat. Only then did she see the boy, a few feet from her at the water's edge. He had not seen her and she stared at him in silence; he was one of the invaders and she knew well who they were. She had often heard her father tell of how they had been raiding Ireland now for many years; of how they had come to the homestead when he was a youth in our Lord's year of 826. That time, however, the people had had warning of their coming and fled to the forests, taking all they could carry, leaving only their crops and homesteads to the pillaging invaders. They came from a far land beyond the sea to the north; the Dubh Gaills they were called. The Black Strangers.

The boy was not tall, but vigorously built, standing braced on his strong brown legs as his eyes followed a flight of duck across the paling sky. She could not see his face but his skin seemed darker than she had ever known, and the hair falling to his shoulders was straight and black. He wore a tunic of grey linen, long-sleeved, and striped with blue and scarlet at the hem. In the leather belt around his waist was the sheath of a long knife.

"But I am *not* afraid," she told herself. "He is only a boy, about twelve years old like me. He is like one of my brothers."

At the thought of her brothers and the death of her family she stirred again restlessly and this time the boy heard her.

The speed of his movement was like an animal. In one bound he was beside her, reaching for the little wicker boat and drawing it to him through the rushes, staring at her fiercely with wide-open dark-blue eyes.

"Who are you?" he demanded.

She stared at him astonished and did not answer.

"Who are you?" he said again. "My father thought to leave no one alive on these islands. Who are you and how are you here?"

Still she stared at him, amazed green eyes on the demanding blue ones. "But you are a Black Stranger —a Viking," she managed to say at last, "and yet you speak my tongue."

"Yes, yes." The dark face creased with impatience. "My father came on viking here before, and took himself a slave. She reared me when my mother died. My father grew to have much regard for her and we speak your tongue often, my father, my cousin and myself. Also my lord Ragnar and others of the older

men have landed here before and passed a winter living among your people. But who are you that I should tell you this! Tell me at once who you are and how you come here. I am Beorn, the Sea King's son, and I would know."

Life flared back into the frightened and exhausted girl. "And I am Ness, daughter of a chief, and I will tell you only if I please!"

She knelt in the boat, her face only a space away from his, and they glared fiercely, anger risen in them both. Slowly the boy moved his hand to the hilt of the long knife. "I am Beorn," he said again, "the son of Anlaf the Sea King, and you will tell me *now!*"

Her eyes followed his hand, and then dropped,

although her breath still came quick and angry. "Very well, I will tell you."

"It is good," said the boy. He crouched at the bow of the little curragh, never moving while she told him how she had hidden in the rushes and escaped the sacking and burning of the village.

"And then? That was the other side of the island. How did you get here?"

She went on to tell him how she had waited patiently for darkness, almost to her waist in water. Then, when the Vikings had started their feasting on the shore and were gathered rejoicing and un-heeding round their fires, she had crept round the island to the little bay on the far side where the curraghs lay in shelter. She had thought to row to the monastery and seek safety with the monks in their tall tower but the Vikings were there before her. It was only the shelter of darkness in a familiar place that had let her escape again to row back, terrified and without thought, to her own island. Here she had lodged the boat deep in the reeds, with no idea of what to do next, and finally in the late night had fallen asleep.

The boy made no comment. He stood up, hold-ing the boat with his foot. "You will get out," he said.

A hot answer rose once more to Ness's lips, but again the boy laid a casual hand on the long knife, and, her mouth tight with anger, she got out.

As she stood up the boy looked at her. Her tunic

was stained and crumpled, her dark-red hair a knotted tangle down to her waist, but her eyes were fierce and her head, he was pleased to find, very nearly as high as his own.

"I like you," he said. "I think you are brave. I will ask my father and you shall be mine."

This time Ness could not hold her temper. "I shall be *yours!*" she flamed at him. "I shall be *yours!* I am myself and I shall belong to *nobody! Nobody!* Least of all to . . . "

The boy rocked gently on the balls of his feet. The blue eyes mocked her. "Least of all to me," he finished for her. "Very well," he went on, his voice indifferent, "very well. You shall not belong to me. We will tell that to my father Anlaf. Come. Will you then die slowly or quickly, he will surely let me choose? I should say quickly were best. Come. Let us go to my father."

Ness thought of the day before. She thought of the horde of warriors rushing over her father's almost defenceless village. She heard again the thin, frantic screaming of the women and children, smelt the bitter smell as the smoke and flames rose above the dry thatch of the huts, and heard above everything else the blood-crazy yelling of the plundering Danes. Her anger faded into hopelessness as she looked at the boy—he was only a boy, but he was a Viking like the others.

"I will be yours," she said tonelessly, and for the first time the young Viking smiled.

"It is good. Now come to my father." He set off so suddenly across the short turf that for a brief moment she was alone. She looked at the boat, but before she could think to move he was beside her again. "*This* is the way to my father." He stood still, close to her, until she turned and went before him along the path which crossed the island.

It was now clear daylight, an early morning in late summer. The small fields above the lake shore had been harvested and the rising sun gilded the stubble above the glitter of the morning lake. In the wood of silver birches in the middle of the island the leaves whispered and rustled with the dryness of the late season. Ness's steps began to lag.

The boy prodded her from behind. "What?" he said mockingly. "Can you not keep the speed of Viking legs?"

Her chin went up and her steps quickened. She would not tell this hateful boy that she could not bear to see the ruins of her family home on the other side of the wood and, when they passed it, she glanced only once and not again.

The quiet fields above the lake, where her father's cattle had browsed only yesterday and where the children had wandered down to play around the water, were alive with men. The huge boats, their masts stepped and their striped sails furled, were drawn up on the narrow strip of shore and the morning life of the Vikings was beginning. Aboard the ships some were working. On the shore and in the fields many

still slept beside their dead fires, wrapped in their big
grey cloaks, the remnants of last night's feasting still
strewn round them. Others sat in groups of three or
four round fresh-lit fires, intent on their morning meal.

Numbers of them got up and crowded round the
boy and girl as they came out of the wood and
down the fields, some laughing, some threatening, all
talking noisily. Ness hesitated and drew back nerv-
ously. The blue eyes derided her again, but without
speaking the boy took her hand in his and led her
down the crowded shore until they stood beneath
the carved serpent-head which crowned the tall prow
of the largest ship.

"What have you there, Beorn? Has one escaped
us? Surely you do not come to ask what to do with
her?"

The voice, speaking in Ness's tongue, came from
above, and with hardly a glance upwards the boy
answered. "You will see, my cousin, both what I
have and what I mean to do. Is my father awake?"
As he spoke, he scrambled up over the shallow side
of the boat, turning to pull Ness after him but
without much care, so that she stumbled over the
rowers' benches and fell into a heap in the well of
the boat.

There was a loud laugh and the same voice spoke
again. "These Irish, they are not people of the sea.
Throw her out and let her try again!"

Bruised and resentful, Ness glared upwards. The
young man who straddled the high foredeck was tall

and broad, handsome, and as fair as Beorn was dark. He laughed uproariously with a couple of men who had drawn close to him, jeering at the girl.

"Throw her back!" the fair young man shouted again to Beorn. "Throw her back and let her try again. That was no way to get into a boat!"

But Beorn dragged her from the well deck and up on to the foredeck, his face dark and angry. "She is mine," he said briefly. "I found her."

"She is yours?" answered the tall one. "Indeed? I would not mind an Irish slave myself, but your father forbade we take them on this raid. Especially I would like one whose hair has tangled with the setting sun. Maybe I will take her." He stretched out a hand and pulled sharply at Ness's hair.

Beorn jerked her aside, and she glanced from the boy to the fair young man. He still smiled at Beorn, but close to him his face was hard and cruel and there was no smile in his fierce light eyes. The boy's face was flushed with open hate and he hustled Ness on towards an awning under the curved prow, his flush deepening at the noisy laughter which followed them.

"I will teach him," he muttered. "When I am older, by the great Hammer of Thor, I will show him what it means to be the son of Anlaf!"

But Anlaf the Sea King, when they reached him, was hardly yet awake, and drowsily uninterested in his son's captive. "Indeed, my son?" He hunched the grey cloak higher around his long form. "You found her?

Then you may keep her. What? Oh, pay no heed to your cousin's teasing. Now leave me. I feasted late and the night watch is not yet over. Go, boy, go, and let me sleep."

For all her sadness and her anger and resentment at being treated like a piece of merchandise, Ness by now was very hungry. When the boy told her to follow him for the morning meal she did so for the first time almost willingly. As they splashed into the shallow water she looked up again and saw the fair young Viking watching them in silence from above.

"I do not like that man," she said. "Who is he?"

The boy glanced sideways at her as if wondering whether he should speak. "He is Helge. I call him cousin, but he is not in truth my cousin, only the son of my father's foster brother, whom he loved. Helge's father was killed and Helge driven away, so my father kept him. He is a great fighter, a great Viking and second to my father in command of the fleet, keeping the night watch. He would rule the fleet should anything happen to my father. I am too young to command." His voice was short and resentful. He paused a moment and then burst out: "I do not like him either. I do not trust him. And I do not think my father trusts him; he watches him carefully."

"Why is he so fair, when all the other men are dark or brown?"

"He is no true Dane. He is from Scania, across the water in the country they call Sweden." Beorn remembered suddenly that he was Anlaf's son and she a captured slave. "I should not talk to you like this! You are my slave, my father said so. Now we shall eat and you shall wait on me."

Ness remembered, too, that she was a chieftain's daughter. "Wait on you I will not! I am used to having my mother's servants wait on me. In this country we do not have the meanness of slavery, for we are Christians, and blessed Patrick, who was himself a slave, taught us that no man should own another. And also my father says . . . said . . . " Her words and her rage faltered together, and her mouth trembled as she looked piteously across at the ruined village, unable to go on.

The boy watched her a long moment in silence. "A Viking does not drive a woman," he said, then. "Come, we will eat together."

While they ate, the watches changed on the longships. She saw Beorn's father emerge from the canopy on the *Great Serpent,* stretching his great length up to the morning sky and shouting for his captains. Never had she seen a man so tall, thin but heavy-shouldered, and moving with the same speed and neatness that marked his son.

The meal over, Ness paused to finger the horn from which she had drunk. She marvelled at the carving on the silver bands which bound it. She had not thought to see barbarians own such a thing of beauty.

The boy got up and left her. "Do not try to run

away while I am gone. I have you well watched and you would have no success," he said. "And think, what if Helge caught you!" The blue eyes widened in mockery, and with a laugh at her rising anger he was gone.

She sat on the familiar short turf, where the fields broke on to the lake shore, and tried to think what she might do. She paid no attention to the Vikings, mustering to the ships in their companies for the day's orders. Her back turned resolutely on her ruined home, she stared down the lake towards the sea. It looked as it had always looked on peaceful summer days; the woods crowding to the edge of the still blue water; the silver birches idling on the small scattered islands and the wildfowl plaintive in the clear air. She was helpless. Her only chance might come at night if she could escape again and reach a boat. Once on the mainland she might be able to find a way through the forests to the fort of her father's brother, who was a lesser King. A shiver of fear struck her; there were wolves in the forest, sometimes even bears. Defiantly her head went up. Far better wolves and bears than Vikings, she told herself, for she would *never* belong to any arrogant infuriating Danish boy.

As she brooded, her eyes on the water, she did not notice that the warriors had begun to gather all together on the lake shore. Their talk and laughter roused her in the end and she turned to watch them. They were excited, laughing, shouting and jostling each other round something on the ground. Curiosity made Ness move closer, peering as best she could, for she would not go too close.

For seconds she gazed speechless at what she saw on the ground in the middle of their circle. Then fury took her. She hurled herself screaming through the astonished Vikings, clawing them aside in her blind rage until she stood shaking above the things which they had heaped on the sandy shore.

"You shall not have them!" she screamed. "You shall not have them! They are ours! That was my father's and this my mother's! The chalice was the Abbot's pride . . . it is *priceless!* It is not yours! You are thieves, villains, robbers!"

Frantically she struck out at the nearest man, struggling to grab his huge sword from its scabbard. Large hands seized her, and there was laughter above her head and some shouts of anger.

A voice cried, in her tongue: "By the Father of Peoples, my uncle, your son has trapped a wildcat! Take her, Beorn, lest we forget that she is yours—our swords may slip!"

Blind with tears and rage, she allowed the boy to drag her out of the crowd, who at once forgot her, intent on their loot.

Still she beat her fists against Beorn. "It is *ours!* I saw my mother's chain of gold, her Cross, it was my father's precious gift to her! I saw——!"

His strong brown hands grasped her wrists. "Peace, girl, peace! By all the gods, have peace! It is all taken in the raid. It is ours now, each man a share according to his rank. My father is only angry that in their excitement they burned the grain store. This also we would take as is our custom. But on this raid, no slaves, but you."

Anger gave way suddenly in Ness to bitter grief. For the first time since she had seen the great striped sails across the lake she collapsed in desperate knowledge of her loss. She laid her head down upon her knees and sobbed with loneliness and misery. The pathetic heap of goods which the Vikings wrangled over seemed suddenly to stand for all that had been taken—father, mother, five brothers and sisters, her home and all her happy childhood.

"I saw my mother's Cross," she moaned over and over and over again, never noticing when the boy left her. She sobbed herself at length into an exhausted sleep, worn out with her grief and her long terrifying night.

It was afternoon when she woke, and the soft late sun was creeping westwards towards the sea. Beside her, the boy Beorn sat sharpening his long knife carefully on a stone. She shivered and sat up, aware that the scene before her had changed, but unable to think for a few moments what was different. Then she realized the shore was empty. The great longships were no longer beached. They stood off a little in the water, held by their banks of oars. Only the serpent boat of the Sea King still lay high up upon the shore. She could not help, even in that moment, but see them beautiful; long, narrow and graceful, tapering in perfection to their high sterns and to the carved heads which topped their bows.

She turned to the boy. "What are they doing?"

"They make ready to sail," Beorn answered.

"But where?"

The boy looked at her. "On the next raid. Where else? There is nothing to keep us here. We have eaten your father's cattle and salted his pigs. We go on to greater treasure now for there was not much here." He breathed lovingly along the gleaming blade of his knife.

Ness stared at him in horror. "And I?"

"You? You will come also. Do you not understand yet that you are mine? You should be proud to belong to Beorn the Sea King's son. I am proud to *be* Beorn."

"Well, I am *not* proud!" she shouted at him. "*Not* proud! And I will not come to see more of my people slaughtered. You are butchers and robbers and I will not come. I hate you and I will not come!"

Beorn hardly appeared to have heard. He went on sharpening his knife, gazing quietly and critically along the edge of the long blade, brilliant with the light of the setting sun. "Not many will be slaughtered," he said at last, as though it did not much interest him. "Only a few monks. And you will come."

"I will not! I will not!"

"You will come. And you may keep this." Without

taking his eyes from his knife, he tossed something at her feet. It was her mother's chain and Cross.

Dumbly she picked it up and held it, running her fingers over the fine carved links, coming in the end to the Cross itself and its small crowned figure. As long as she could remember her mother, she had fingered it thus, warm about her neck. She looked up at the boy, at a loss for words, too grateful to be angry, and yet still too angry to be properly grateful.

She still had found no words, when, in answer to a signal from his father's ship, Beorn stood up and sheathed his knife. "You will come," he said.

She slipped the chain over her head and looked in baffled fury at his back. In silence, she followed him.

CHAPTER TWO

THE EVENING WIND was freshening as the long procession of ships drove from the river mouth into the wide bay, and in the gathering darkness turned southwards along the wild and rocky coast of western Ireland. Despairingly, Ness stood on the high stern deck and peered through the dusk at the narrow inlet which led to the fort of her father's brother. Only this summer she had sailed there with her family. Now she watched the familiar coastline vanish into the grey evening, and turned resignedly to face her captivity.

In the bustle which filled the ship as orders were given for the coming raid no one paid much heed to her. Now that the *Great Serpent* was at sea, the tent of Anlaf was pitched in the wide well deck, and here he sat on his carved stool with Helge and the other captains gathered around him, discussing their plans. About them hovered Beorn, listening to every word and desperately anxious to be one of them. The night was well gone before they separated; Helge to stand alone on his night watch and Anlaf to roll himself in his great cloak and take what sleep was left.

Beorn looked at last at the shivering girl, crouched in the well to try and escape the cold night wind. "Sleep," he said. "You will be early awake."

She glared at him. "I am too cold to sleep."

"Oh—ho! The Irish blood is thin and cold! Take this. I do not need it—I am a Viking!" He tossed her his cloak.

"My blood is as good as yours, and I do not need your cloak!"

"It is as you say." Beorn threw himself indifferently beside his father, and seemed to sleep at once.

In the dim starlight Ness watched him for a long time, cold and wakeful, looking from him to the warm cloak lying neglected on the deck. At last she stretched out a hand and pulled it towards her where she huddled against the boards, dragging it gratefully over her when she saw the boy did not move. As she snuggled into its warm rough folds, the voice of Helge spoke acidly from the deck above.

"Ah!" he said. "So your Irish pride is not enough to keep you warm. It would be wise to remember that pride is not for slaves. You would get no cloak from me!"

Ness did not answer, but edged a little closer to Beorn and his father, for with Helge she was afraid. Pride or no, she stayed wrapped in the cloak, watching the brilliant stars of the clear night and listening to the soft chorus of unfamiliar creaks and strains and the hiss and slap of the night sea, as the *Great*

Serpent drove steadily to the south under her huge square sail.

She must have slept, for when she woke, with movement all around her, it was morning. A grey light was breaking to a cool green dawn over a calm and silent sea, on which the fleet of longships rested at anchor. Shivering and stiff, she shook off her cloak and went up on to the deck to look about her, keeping carefully out of the way of the hurrying warriors who were checking their arms and unhooking their shining shields from where they hung above the oar bench.

The ships lay some distance out from the coast, still grey and shadowy before the coming of the sun. It was a cruel coast with great mountains tumbling to the water and long lines of steep and wicked-looking cliffs. Nearer at hand, to the seaward side, there was a solitary island. It was more a tall narrow chimney of rock than an island, pointing like a dark finger into the pearling sky.

Now the Vikings were gathered in their arms on the fore and stern decks. This, however, was only on the *Great Serpent* and two other boats which lay near her. On the rest, the men crowded only to watch. They were all excited but quiet, the armed ones looking to Helge and Anlaf for their orders and dropping quickly into the three small boats lowered from the ship's side. Ness sought Beorn, who hovered, as always, round the fighting men.

"What do they do?" she asked, mystified. "What —where do they go? There is not a living soul at hand!" She stared all round, from the bleak distant coast to the dark chimney of rock.

"Is there not?" Beorn's blue eyes were derisive. "There you are wrong. It seems I know more of your country than you do yourself. You see that rock? Perched upon the top is one of the richest monasteries in Ireland. Did you not know? A few old men, seated helpless on their treasure. It is ours for the taking!"

"It is not possible!" Ness stared unbelievingly. "How did they get up? And how will you get up?"

"You will see!" Like all the Vikings, the boy was excited and confident.

"I do not believe you. How do you know there is a monastery there?"

The boy took his eyes from the small boats and looked at her with pity and condescension. "How did my father know," he asked her bitingly, "that there was a monastery on the shores of your lake? Do you think he found it just by chance? How did he know exactly the course to steer that he might reach this rock this morning? Did you not know that there are people who would do *anything* for gold?"

Ness stared at him appalled. "Someone from Ireland *told* him? For gold? Not the Irish slave you told me of? She did not tell—not a woman?"

"Macha? No, no. She would not tell a thing like

that, she would tell my father he should not go. She
still holds her love for Ireland, even though she has
not seen it since my father was a youth. No, but
there is always someone who will tell for gold. Or
freedom."

The girl had no more to say. She was so shocked
that someone would sell her country and her country's treasure for the sake of gold that she could only
stare in silence at the small boats which crept across
the slate-blue water. The sun topped the mountains
behind them; the dark sea turned to a sheet of gold
and the tall finger of shadowed rock to a fragile
castle of pale greening stone round which the seabirds
wheeled and drifted. The boats vanished behind the

base of the pillar and Ness looked up to the top of it. As the sunlight slowly strengthened, she was able to see at last what the shadows had concealed: small figures moving among the highest points of rock.

Pity for the defenceless monks seized her. "You cannot do it!" she cried to Beorn. "You cannot do it! You say you are brave and glorious fighters, fierce Vikings! How is it brave to kill a handful of defenceless men, many of them old and none of them warriors? I say that you are cowards! You will only fight when you can kill easily and then steal above the bodies of the dead! You are *cowards*, cowards!"

Beorn raised his eyebrows. "It would not be wise to let Helge hear you speak like that. His sword already lies uneasy in its scabbard at the thought of you. But cowards . . . " He was quite unruffled. "I do not think so. We can fight when it is needed, but we are not here to fight. We are on viking, girl, and it is a sport. When I creep across the marshes in the dawn, taking my blunted arrows to bring down the wildfowl for their rich flesh, am I a coward because the birds cannot strike back? Do I go back home with my bow unslung and stay hungry for pity that my arrows pierce the birds in death? Have sense, girl, it is the same thing on viking. We come for what we can get."

"It is *not* the same thing! These are people, *people*, not birds. Our God teaches that a man's life is sacred——"

"Oh, your God! We have heard a lot about your

God. Macha, the Irishwoman, is what do you call it? A Christian. She also would talk to me of love and softness and all such foolishness. Your God is a fine one for women and old men but of no use to warriors."

"You are so proud, I wonder your Macha bothers to tell you anything. She must see it is a waste of time." Ness stared helplessly at his calm, satisfied face and groped for words to touch him. She could only speak of what she knew. "My father was tall and strong. In all the gatherings he could outrun and out-wrestle all who challenged him. When need be he was a great warrior, too. But he was a Christian and with his strength he was most wise and gentle." She closed her eyes with a pang of desperate grief for her tall, handsome father, so mighty a man among men, but so wise and gentle and endlessly patient to a troubled child. Her mouth trembled as she finished, not quite clear herself in what she said, but knowing it to be true. "Sometimes it is stronger to be gentle."

Beorn dismissed her with a gesture. "Women's talk!" he said, and laughed again, suddenly yelling out in excitement. "There goes the first. My father is there. Ho! This will make a good splash!"

Dumb with horror, Ness watched as a tiny body, arms and legs wide, hurtled from the top of the rock, falling, falling down through the pale sunlight to vanish in the end with hardly a splash into the shining sea. One after another the small puppets came down, dark against the glittering day, and round them the frightened seabirds wheeled and shrieked, with the sun on their white wings.

Ness stared and licked her parched lips. She turned her head and stared all round her, trying to understand that a morning of such beauty could hold such frightfulness. The boy beside her laughed and shouted praises of his father and his clever cousin. Around them, all the Vikings shouted too, their excitement rising with each falling body, for they had heard a lot about the loot which would fall into their hands from this killing; and only a handful of men needed for it. Indeed Anlaf was a clever leader. They were delighted, and looked hungrily now to their morning meal when the men came back after a job well done.

Beorn saw Ness's stricken face and laughed aloud. "Oh, ho, my chieftain's daughter, you will have to learn to be less squeamish when you belong to a Sea King's son. And I shall be a Sea King one day myself and expect you to be proud of me. It is good sport to be on viking, is it not? What would your women's God think of this?"

Ness felt too sick to answer him. She walked away abruptly and went to the stern of the boat as far as she could go, standing with her arm round the spiralling tail of the *Great Serpent*. She looked backwards to where the sea ran deep into the land, a shining inlet between the dark mountains along its sides. Looking at the empty country, she could pretend that she was alone and grope in her horrified mind for the words of the prayers which she knew she should say for the souls of the poor dead monks. Only now did she remember that she had never thought to pray for her family. Nor could she, for she did not yet believe that they were gone.

After a long time, she heard the small boats bumping against the *Great Serpent* as they came back one by one. She heard the noisy clamour, the laughter and the boisterous shouting of the successful raiders. She heard the faint click of metal away behind her as the bags of loot were dumped on the deck. She would not turn round to look. Then she heard a voice that could not belong to any Viking; an old voice and soft, that she could barely hear, speaking in her own tongue and asking for gentleness and pity.

She whipped round then. "No use to ask these murderers for pity," she began to shout. Then she stopped, the words dead on her lips. The voice had come from a very old man, frail and small, his long white hair and beard trailing down over his shapeless habit. His seamed old face was waxen and his eyes closed painfully as if the light troubled him. But though he stumbled often and seemed unsteady on his feet, he faced the ring of noisy men with quietness and dignity.

Ness came slowly forward along the length of the ship to where Helge stood before the old man. Helge was flushed and noisy with excitement, his blue eyes prominent and wild. Blood gleamed sticky in his fair hair and down the front of his leather vest.

"Ah, little slave of my cousin," he cried in Irish, "see what a strange old bird we have plucked from his nest on the rock! We found him sealed in a little hut. Thirty years he says he spent there, thirty years in a little dark hut when the gods have given us the wind and the sea and the world for our taking! Thirty years—he says his God gave him peace in his little hut, but I thought it time he saw the world and learnt what he has missed. He can say his prayers over us instead and bring us good fortune. He shall be our mascot. Hey, old man!" He prodded the hermit with the shaft of his axe and the old man tottered unsteadily.

Ness leapt to support him. "Peace, my father," she said softly, "and I beg your blessing. I am captive like you and I will do all I can to help you."

The old man peered at her helplessly. "Ah, my child, I do not see you well. The years of darkness have taken my sight, but your voice is young. You are but a child? Then have no care for me. See to it that you escape these people. I do not know who or what they are, but they are evil."

"What are you whispering about?" yelled Helge. "I will not have you weaving spells together against us. Beorn, I charge you see they have no secret talk or when you seek your slave you may find her in the sea! He is our charm of good fortune, the ancient one. He shall bring us good luck, good viking and much treasure!" He turned and shouted again to the Vikings in their own language and loud laughter and cheers rose from the excited men.

Ness hurled herself out in front of them. "Good luck!" she cried. "Good luck! This is the most terrible thing you have done yet, to wrench this holy ancient from his cell and turn him loose among heathens and barbarians. He were better dead with all the rest. It will bring you no luck at all!"

In the clear sunlight her red hair blazed like fire above her angry face and her green eyes flashed around the circle of men, while her fists clenched and unclenched themselves as though, with her small strength, she was ready to attack any one of them. "I will tell you now," she went on, "it will bring you no good fortune. It will bring a curse on you, this thing you have done today. Nothing will go well for you, for you have offended our God to whom this old one had given his life. You will see; there will be *no* luck."

Beorn forgot his enmity with Helge in the richness of the joke. They clapped each other on the back and shouted her words derisively to the men in their own language, rolling with mirth at the idea that this frail old creature, or even his God, could bring misfortune to a host of Vikings. The men joined willingly in the laughter and mockery, and in a few moments Ness would have been shouted down and her curse forgotten.

Then, for the first time since the raid, she caught sight of Anlaf. He had come aboard among the last and held back from the circle round the hermit.

Ness flung out a triumphant arm. "See!" she cried. "See! Already your Sea King is wounded. Already the ill fortune has come."

There was no need now for anyone to repeat her words, for the men understood her well enough when they turned and looked at Anlaf. Their laughter died and doubt crept over their faces. Their leader was deathly pale, his vest and tunic drenched with blood still seeping strongly from a wounded shoulder.

He sensed their dismay and cried at once that it was nothing. "Nothing at all but a flesh wound with much blood. There was a young shaveling there who attacked me with a knife. By Thor's hammer, he fought well for a man who teaches love! Now get away from all this foolish talk and to your food. I will have my wound dressed and then we will share our spoils and turn to the next picking on the way home. We have done well today, indeed that must be the richest rock in Ireland. Now let me by."

Reassured, the men dispersed to gather in groups for the morning meal, recounting their triumphs and looking forward to their food.

Ness settled the old man in the well as comfortably as she could, and sat down at his feet, nor would she move from there despite all Helge's threats. When Helge threatened, Beorn stayed close.

"Though not," thought Ness bitterly, "that he cares

what happens to me. It is simply that he will not allow Helge to threaten anything he owns."

Nor did he fail to jibe at her, his blue eyes bright with malicious fun. "The old one belongs, you say, to your God. Well, let us see your God take him back from us and set him once more on his rock!" He laughed with great pleasure at his own jest, and stretched his strong brown legs in the sun.

Ness fingered the Cross at her neck and tried to remember that she should pray for her enemies as well as for the dead she loved. She looked at the handsome boy lying carelessly at her feet and the only prayer that would come into her mind was one for vengeance.

"You will see," she said, with an effort to speak quietly. "His God will not fail him."

Beorn did not even bother to answer.

CHAPTER THREE

"WE WILL GO home by the North Route," Anlaf said to his son the next day. "The year grows late and it may be wild, but there is a monastery there among the small islands that should be well worth the picking."

"Wild?" Beorn looked around him. Since the fair, clear dawn of the previous day, the level sunlit sea and the high blue sky had been like those of midsummer. "If this weather holds," he said, "the rowers may be glad to see a little wildness. What is the matter, my father, does your shoulder pain you?"

"A little," answered the Sea King. "It is nothing," he said, but he moved restlessly on his stool.

Along the rowing benches the Vikings laboured at their oars, their tunics thrown aside and the sweat beading the edges of their hair and running down their broad backs. Irritable from their day and night of feasting, they cursed the sudden unseasonable weather which drove them so hard. It was their custom to sail on viking when the crops were harvested and the late summer days grew cool, with fresh

30

second misfortune

Sails were not sailing.

autumn winds to fill the great sails and help the rowers.

Now there was no wind. Nor was there on the next day nor the next, and the boats progressed slowly under the burning sun that parched their tongues beyond the limits of their water.

"Can we not go ashore, my father," asked Beorn, "and let the men rest until this windless heat has passed?"

"This coast is rocks, rocks, rocks, there is nowhere we could beach. In any case we are not equipped for a big battle which we may well run into if we land anywhere we do not know. I think it too great a risk."

Clasping his wounded shoulder as if it troubled him, he continued to stare at the barren coast that crept so slowly past, and Beorn wandered back to the well deck where Ness still sat much of the day beside the ancient hermit. The old man did not complain of the heat, nor of anything else. He sat patiently through the long, blazing days, blinking in the unaccustomed light and taking gratefully a little of what food and drink Ness brought to him. He spoke seldom, as if the effort of living in such strange surroundings was as much as he could manage. Tired with the effort of rowing in the blistering heat, the men no longer bothered to pay him any attention, but he was much in their minds. *Q. 13. why?*

It was on the third day that Ness came flying to Beorn where he sat with his father. "Do you know what one of the men told me," she burst out, "the one they call Knot Beard who speaks my tongue? They all say the hermit's curse is growing on the boat; they say he has brought this terrible heat and killed the wind that the longships may never return to their own land. They say that Christian priests always bring bad weather luck. They say . . . " She stopped in confusion and looked at the Sea King in embarrassment.

"They say," he finished for her quietly, "that Anlaf is dying."

His face indeed was deadly pale and he did not move around the ship as he had previously done but left the supervision to Helge and Ragnar, his second captain. He stayed beneath his awning, resting the shoulder, which obviously gave him great pain, as best he could.

"Well," he went on now, "you may tell them that he is not dead *yet* and it will be unwise for any man to behave as though he is. What does Helge say about these stories of his old man of good fortune?"

"I know," interrupted Beorn. "I have heard all this." He shot a crushing glance at Ness. "The old man is Helge's charm, so Helge says these tales are nonsense. The great god Niord rules the wind and sea and shall any old man upset him? Myself, I would throw the old man into the sea and keep the men happy, but Helge is obstinate—and you know, my father, what Helge is like when he is obstinate. He would die now before he would throw the old one overboard, for all

Helge's scared of pride?

he may be terrified at heart. I expect he fingers Thor's hammer round his neck, and calls for protection every hour the ancient stays on board!"

Anlaf smiled faintly, but Ness stared at Beorn with big, horrified eyes. "You could not throw him in the sea. Did I not say evil would come simply for his capture? It is the old man's God you have offended, it would not help to do him more harm."

Beorn shrugged. "How could *you* know, and what is one old man to a contented ship? Who knows, the men may be right!"

"I do know! I do know! Our God cares for those who serve Him. If you do not wish to anger Him further, then put the old man ashore somewhere where there are people. Then he may be led back to his own way of life."

"And risk our necks going ashore with a praying ancient!"

"Do not bait her, Beorn, my son," said Anlaf wearily. "I think she is a good child. She puts me much in mind of Macha who has grown so dear to us, with all her talk, too, of her loving God. You must mind the child against Helge when . . . " He stopped.

The boy's head flashed round. "When what? When what, my father?"

"Nothing," Anlaf answered. "Nothing."

And with that, Beorn had to be content, but Ness watched his anxious eyes on his father, and found place for pity, even though she hated him, a Viking boy. "He is only a child as I am for all his proud ways," she thought, "and I know well what it is to lose my father." So she was unusually kind to him as they moved round the boat and Beorn looked at her with suspicion, his dark face creased uncertainly, ready to flare with anger in his Viking pride if she dared to pity him.

Helge slept through the hot hours of the day watch, while talk and tension mounted in the slow-moving boat. When at evening he emerged, it was to scowls and angry faces.

"Throw the old one in the sea!" They crowded to the stern of the boat where he stood, handsome and stubborn.

"Feed him to the gulls!" they shouted.

"Kill him and bring the wind!"

"Let us sacrifice the old man himself to Niord!"

"Kill the old one of ill fortune! Bring the wind!"

Underneath the shouting they whispered the thing they dared not shout. "The Sea King dies," they said.

Ness stared at them from where she stood protectively beside the indifferent old man. "I do not understand," she said.

When Beorn told her what they said, she answered bitingly: "Why do they tell Helge to kill him? If they are so afraid, why do they not kill him themselves? He is an old man and helpless, and they are Vikings. They should be able to manage him."

For one moment, she thought the boy would hit her. Then he answered her coldly, as if to show her that loss of temper with a girl would be beneath him.

"Because," he said, "they fear Helge more than they fear the gods. What Helge says is his, *is* his, and they dare not move. He is too ready with his sword. They will not do anything unless he bids them."

Helge would not bid them. "Get to your oars!" he shouted, his fair face flushed with sleep and anger. "Go to your oars and talk no more like old women! What can this ancient do against our gods? If we suffer misfortune, it is their doing and we must accept it. Get to your places, we will sacrifice to Niord, and get good luck—a wind and fresh health for our Sea King! All will be well!"

But, despite the sacrifice to Niord, their fortune did not change. The next day dawned with the same settled heat and in his tent Anlaf the Sea King burned with fever. All his great Viking courage could not raise him from his bed.

"It is nothing," he said to Beorn. "The wound is slow to heal. It is nothing."

"Indeed, my father, it is nothing," answered the boy; but his anxious face grew pale as his father's.

Along the rowing benches, and where the watch-off gathered on the sterndeck, the muttering grew to an angry growl. Scores of fierce eyes glared along the sunbaked boat to where the old hermit sat with eyes closed against the sun. It no longer mattered to him where his body was. His brutal removal from the lonely silence of his hermitage had proved too much for his old mind. Indifferent to all the trouble he was causing, he now sat isolated in his wandering thoughts, solitary as he had been in his beehive hut among the pinnacles of rock. The face he turned upon the growling men was empty and serene.

It was on the evening of this day that they discovered themselves to be without meat. Below the deckboards of the boat lay the long vats of salted meat that should provide them for the voyage. To this they added what they could capture on the way, such as the fine pigs owned by Ness's father. This should make the meal for the weary Vikings coming off the hot day's watch, wiping away the sweat of the blistering hours, thirsty, tired and anxious for the last meal of the evening.

"It is rotten!" came the sudden cry. "All of it! There is nothing. All our meat is gone!"

Helge thrust aside the men who rushed and clamoured to peer down into the vats. "It cannot be!" he cried. "It was good yesterday!"

He stood silent with all the others, gazing down into the curdled slimy mass that should have fed them until they reached home.

Ness peered between their crowded legs and then drew back, smitten by a pang of something close to fear. In her rage at the capture of the hermit, she had shouted and threatened the Vikings with the vengeance of her God. But her secret prayers had been much more for the life and safety of the poor old man. Now she watched in amazement as her wild words came slowly true: Anlaf was sinking towards death, and now the food supply was gone. Was God indeed answering her shouts for vengeance?

She blessed herself a little fearfully and caught Beorn's eyes upon her, for the first time without pride or mockery. Vengeance from the gods was something he understood well.

The men were wilder than ever.

"It is the old one!" they shouted.

"He has cursed us as the child said he would!"

"He is our ill luck!" They all shouted together.

"And the Sea King dies," they whispered beneath the shouting.

"Quiet!" yelled Helge. "It is the heat, what else? Just as it is the heat that fevers the Sea King's wound. Will I throw the ancient in the sea and show us all up as old women, frightened by an old man parted from his wits! Signal the boats nearby and let us see what food we have between us!"

They had practically none. All the longships were in the same plight as the *Great Serpent,* and in all of them, too, water was running low.

The men swarmed and grumbled. "Do we row home in this heat, by the hard North Route, on oatmeal?"

Helge pushed through them and in the Sea King's tent he talked to Ragnar. They tried to talk with Anlaf but he gazed at them now with hazy fevered eyes, his wits as lost as the old man's in the well deck. It was left to them to decide what they must do.

"We must seek a beach and go ashore for food and water," said Helge.

"Then we must go where there are people, and that is a danger. We are only lightly armed for viking, and we cannot fight great numbers. It seems a foolish risk to kill one half of the men that we may feed the other."

"We must try to *buy*. We will send gold and valuables to offer."

"We should do it soon." Ragnar was an older man and had been on viking here before. "The country is a little milder north of here, and there are valleys between the mountains, and villages. Farther on it grows wild again and we may not get another chance."

"We will send only a few men who speak the tongue," said Helge, "and then the villagers will not feel themselves threatened. Take some of the monastery spoils and pay them well. We should get enough meat to see us to this island in the north where the monks, we are told, breed cattle fat and lazy as themselves."

It was late morning when they found themselves opposite a long pale beach, fronting a lush valley between gently sloping hills. Trees and bushes hid any signs of a village but on the lower mountain slopes they made out the small shapes of browsing cattle.

"This is our place!" cried Helge. "Go gently with these people. When you have the meat, signal us from the shore, and we will send boats to carry it."

The four carefully picked men left the longship and rowed to the stretch of yellow sand below the green fields. From the sea, the others watched their distant figures drag the boat up the beach and disappear into the trees. All day long they waited for them to come back, but the limpid green of the evening sky faded into purple and then into darkness above the mountains and still there was no sign of them.

Beorn, like everyone else, haunted the foredeck, from where he watched the shore. But he moved restlessly between there and his father's tent, where the Sea King tossed and muttered and his failing eyes roamed endlessly over everything and saw nothing.

Backwards and forwards, Ness followed him. "What do you think has happened?" she asked. Deep in her heart she prayed for some miracle that would overthrow these ships and set her back among the soft hills and the green fields at which she had stared so yearningly all day.

"What do *you* think has happened?" the boy answered irritably. "They are your people."

"Well, I think they have been killed!" flashed Ness. "I think my people would sell *nothing* to those who came to buy with their country's stolen treasures."

"They would be glad to get them back for a few sides of beef. And, besides, no handful of peasants could kill four Vikings!"

Ness tossed her head.

Far on into the night, the small boat bumped softly against the *Great Serpent's* side. Only one man was dragged aboard, desperately wounded and almost spent. Through dying lips he whispered his story. Seeing only four of the Black Strangers, the villagers had not been hostile until the sacks were opened and they saw what had been brought in exchange for the cattle. They had then fallen immediately upon the Vikings and slaughtered them. Ness, gathering what had happened from the sight of the dying, empty-handed man, looked at Beorn but he would not meet her eyes.

This one man, left for dead, had managed somehow to crawl in darkness to the rowing-boat and reach the *Great Serpent*. Before he died he was able to assure Helge that there was nothing there other than a village with no very large force of men.

"Then we go in strength," cried the angered Helge. "What they will not give, we shall have to take!"

Ragnar shook his head. "I think, my friend, it was foolish to send their own treasures. They are roused now, and ready for us. We cannot take them by surprise and our force is diminished."

"And what would you have me send them? Danish silver? Remember, Ragnar, we are Vikings. If they number ten to one of us, we can hold these Irish."

Ness plucked at Beorn's sleeve but he stared at the deck, his brown face turned away, and would not tell her what they said, only that they were to attack the Irish village in force.

"Come, Ragnar," said Helge again, "let us get ready for our raid. Who knows what we may pick up!"

But the men had no heart for the venture and when Helge ordered them to be ready at dawn there was much anger against him and his old hermit. They put at his door their failure to buy food and now they felt that they went off to fight under the shadow of a curse without hope of success.

"First kill the old one!" they cried.

"Save us and save the Sea King!" They no longer whispered that he was dying.

"Take away the curse of the hermit!"

"Kill him!"

Now when they attacked him about the hermit Helge began to look uneasy. Like Ness, he had begun to think on the disasters which had followed them since the capture of the old man. But his obstinacy overrode his fears and doubts, and fair, strong and furious he stood up before them.

"Are you Vikings," he yelled at them, "or a pack of babes around your mother's skirts? Since when did you fear death? A Viking dies only on the day appointed and dies in shame if he does not die in arms! So gather your arms and be ready, I say, and no more of this talk. Call upon Tyr to give you spirit and Thor to give you strength and forget the mumblings of old men and the threats of their feeble God!"

In the dawn of the next day, the *Great Serpent* lay off the coast with Ragnar and a handful of men to guard the dying Anlaf and the children. The rest of the longships were run ashore on the beach, the rowers staying at the benches so that they might leave again at great speed if necessary.

There were no defenders on the shore, and the orderly column of warriors disappeared into the trees as the four men had done. In the strengthening heat of the day, the watchers stood on the high foredeck of the *Great Serpent* and waited for their victorious return.

"It grows hot again," said Beorn, "and my father's fever runs high. I wish this were over and we could set to sea. Even by oar, it is cooler for him there."

"This will not take long," Ragnar answered confidently, and even as he spoke the first of the returning Vikings burst from the trees.

"Ragnar!" Beorn's voice was hoarse with shock. "Ragnar! What is *wrong!*"

"I do not know! I do not know! There must have been more here than a handful of peasants! Oh, why am I left with children and the dying!"

The Vikings charged down the shore, disorganized and desperately depleted; a mere handful of the body of fighting men that had gone out. Some reached the boats in safety. Others fell as they ran under the hail of arrows which pursued them from an enemy hidden among the trees. As fast as possible, the rowers took the boats to sea; the last of the fighters and the slow-moving wounded splashing through the shallows to be dragged on board by their fellows.

As the beach cleared, the Irish showed themselves,

massing on the shore in their hundreds, screaming their terrible war cry and continuing to shower the fleeing Vikings with their arrows for as long as they could reach them.

"Oh!" cried Ness, wild with delight at the success of her people. "Oh, that was well done!"

Had the furious Beorn not held her, she would have leapt thoughtless over the side, indifferent to the space of water that lay between her and her friends.

"Now!" She wriggled fiercely in the boy's grasp and turned to face him, her green eyes blazing with triumph. "Now do you see what happens when Vikings really have to *fight!*"

The boy stood silent a moment, his eyes brooding on the advancing longships. Then he lifted his head proudly and turned away from Ness, dropping his hands from her arms. "It is fair," he said. "A good Viking knows when to admit defeat."

Ness stamped with rage. It was all the more maddening that she could not anger him as she knew her remark was *not* fair. It was obvious that the Vikings had been attacked by a force far greater than their own. There must have been a fort nearby, that of a chieftain or even a king, to whom the villagers had gone for help.

When the men came back on board the *Great Serpent* they were not so calm about their defeat. Bloodstained, wounded and dishevelled, they raged and shouted round the serene old man in the well

deck. Now they were certain he was the cause of all
their misfortunes. So certain that they held away from
him in superstitious fear, but Helge, they shouted,
must get rid of him.

Helge himself was much the worse for battle, his
tunic torn and soaked in blood, his fair hair matted
from a head wound just below his helm. In spite of
terrible odds, he had led his men and fought himself
with all the valour of a true Viking. The hardest
decision he had made was the one to retreat and
now he stood before his angry warriors, baffled and
confused, able only to yell at them that he would
think on what they said. He was almost as frightened as they.

In the tent he tried to discuss it with Ragnar. "It
seems to me there is truth in what they say. I think
the gods have forsaken us since I brought this ancient on board, and yet . . . "

"And yet you fear now to kill him lest it is *his*
God you are offending."

They turned in sharp surprise at Anlaf's voice.
They had forgotten him in their anxiety, used by
now to his fevered ramblings. Now they saw that the
fevered look had left his face, but Ragnar, his old
friend, looked with sorrow at the sharpened look of
death which had come to take its place.

Anlaf's eyes were no longer wild and his thin
voice was calm and quiet. "Is that not so, Helge?"

"Yes, yes, my uncle! How did you know? I do not
know by now whose god I have offended to bring us

these disasters. Ours, by having this Christian priest on board our ship—or have I offended the old man's God as that child of Beorn's said I would. I only did it for a jest and now look where it has brought us all!"

Helge ran his hands despairingly through his bloody hair, wincing as his careless fingers dragged his wound.

The strange light voice of Anlaf spoke again. "I am close to death now," he said, "and I have no idea who is right, though I have listened long to Macha and know of her Christian God. But I shall die by the gods I have lived with; the gods of my fathers before me. Still, I think it wise that you get the old man away, Helge. Do not kill him. Put him ashore with food and drink or soon the men will kill you."

Ness tugged at Beorn on the fringe of the group and he whispered to her what his father had said.

"But the old man is simple," she breathed, knowing she had no place to speak. "He has lost his wits. He cannot care for himself."

"Hold your tongue!" snarled Helge, but Anlaf had heard her.

"Then," he said faintly, "his plight will not trouble him."

Ness worried still at Beorn when the others had left and they sat on the ground beside the dying chieftain, now seemingly asleep.

"How can they do it? The poor man. It would have been kinder to kill him in the first place. He will have a wretched death."

Even Beorn's proud confidence was confused and shaken by the events of the past few days and his answer was without much of his usual arrogance. "As my father says, his plight will not trouble him." He gathered himself to attack, knowing by now where he could wound her. "And what matter whether he is alive or dead? I think, myself, that Helge loses his head. What harm can that old weakling do? Weak as the God he serves, they cannot harm us! I tell you He is a women's God." Now he had talked himself to confidence again. "We have robbed enough monasteries by now to learn that those who serve Him are weaklings all! That is why we have no use but to laugh at your God. Helge loses his head!"

Cold anger rose in Ness. "And what," she asked him, clearly and cruelly, "what about the young monk who has killed your father?"

What does Anlaf tell to do with the old man?

The blue eyes blazed on her in a confusion of fury and grief. "An odd one, an odd one!" he shouted, and jumped up to lean over the rail, his eyes fixed on the sea below him.

Ness followed more slowly, her mind filling with the memory of long days that now seemed for ever summer. Days spent sitting with the other island children about the feet of Brother Feredach in the Abbey on the lake shore, listening to the endless tales of the saints and scholars who had made the golden age of Ireland and taken the light of Christianity through hardship and danger to the farthest corners of an abandoned Europe. Crowding to her mind came tales of courage and endurance and holiness and strength, the names of men who had turned away even from kingdoms to give their strength and valour to God. Weaklings!

"Columcille!" she shouted suddenly at the astonished boy. "Columcille. He was born an O'Neill of Ulster, heir to the High King himself, yet he left it all for God. A mighty man as tall as your father and so great a warrior that he was fifteen years a priest, yet still could not forget it, and drew the sword in anger." She saw that she had got the boy's unwilling attention; he was startled at her vehemence and drawn, in spite of himself, by what she said.

"He had an argument," she went on more quietly, "with his master Finnian over a copy of the Gospel. The High King gave the ruling to Finnian, and the warrior in Columcille grew greater than the priest.

He mustered the O'Neills against the followers of the High King, and led them into bloody battle that left three thousand slain."

This was language Beorn could understand. "And you say he was a priest? What then?"

"Then the warrior remembered that he was a priest." Ness spoke in the words of Brother Feredach. "And the deaths lay heavy on his soul. He said he would leave Ireland and go to the pagan country of Dalriada, to gather for God one soul for every one he led to death. He went to Iona, the holy island, the first one where he could climb the highest hill and not see Ireland. That was his penance."

Penance did not interest Beorn so much. "Three thousand slain," he repeated. "That was indeed a battle. Three thousand slain! And you say he was a priest?" He shook his head, and his eyes turned thoughtfully to the old man.

Throughout that day and night the Vikings rowed on in the sweltering heat until morning showed them that they would soon be clearing Ireland. Helge signalled that the *Great Serpent* was closing in to the shore, and down into a small boat they bundled the smiling, unprotesting old man. He did not even understand when Ness knelt before him and asked him for his blessing.

Along the *Great Serpent's* side the Vikings cheered and shouted. Now the ill luck would leave the fleet —or what was left of it, for in the long days of rowing, many had fallen behind and after the battle the number of men was greatly reduced. They shouted with delight and tossed their leather caps into the air when they saw Helge leave the hunched old figure on the ground and place beside it all the meal and water they could spare.

"Now we are free!" they cried as he climbed back on board.

"Now we will have good fortune!"

"Now the Sea King will recover!"

Beorn had recovered his confidence with the rest of them, and his face reflected the fresh hopes of the men. Jubilantly he dug the silent Ness in the ribs. "There he goes," he cried. "Now where is his powerful God to save him, for he will surely die with no one to help him. I thought your God was to care for him?"

Sick with sadness, Ness closed her fingers round her Cross and groped for the faith that now seemed to be all she had left in the world. This time it was her mother's words that came to her, offered so often in comfort for childish disappointments.

"We must not question His way of doing things," she said painfully. "Sometimes we do not understand, but if we wait a little maybe we shall see."

Beorn laughed aloud and turned back to the rejoicing men. In spite of another hot and windless morning, they bent themselves to their oars with a vigour and cheerfulness they had not shown since they rowed away from the island monastery.

By the *Great Serpent's* tail, Ness stood in tears.

Q. All she has in the world is her faith.

The small loss of the old man seemed to bring her at last to hopeless understanding of the greater loss of all her family. She did not move until the small white figure on the ground had merged into the green fields and they, in turn, into the blue haze which was the last she saw of her country.

Late in the same night, the men still rowed with their fresh hope and vigour, sure that the curse was ended and all would now be well. But in the starlit darkness, Anlaf the Sea King called for his son and for Helge. He bade them raise him from his bed and over his shaking, helpless body he bade them draw on all his clothes and armour. With Ragnar's help, they supported him to where his carved stool had been placed high on the foredeck beneath the serpent's head. Here his heavy helm was put on, slipping down over the head grown too frail to hold it. On his left arm they hung his great round burnished shield, and in his limp right hand they laid his mighty axe, with which he had flailed into all the battles of his life. Somehow he bore the crushing weight. Now, a Viking fully armed upon his ship, he would die in honour.

Through the long dark night, while fear and superstition raced like fever through the boat, Anlaf sat on his carved stool beneath the head of his great serpent and turned his ashen face upon the sky. He watched for the long shaft of light and the Valkyrie riding her white steed, come to summon him to the proud tables of Valhalla.

As the first stars paled before the oncoming day, he trembled suddenly and lifted up his axe and shining shield towards the sky. Life left his hands and the weapons clattered to the deck.

The Valkyrie had come and Anlaf the Sea King had joined the warriors of Odin.

CHAPTER FOUR

NOW HELGE TOOK his new place of authority over the Vikings, but nothing was as he had
planned it. He sat on the foredeck and glared mood-
ily at the tent where Anlaf lay waiting for burial when
they should make landfall. All the years of his man-
hood he had looked to this day when Anlaf would be
dead and the Sea King's power in his hands. He took
no heed of Beorn; the boy could be dealt with before
he grew old enough to be a threat.

Lately, Helge had even begun to plan secretly to
kill Anlaf, and his good looks and fierce valour in
battle had led a certain number of the men to follow
him. Now the day was here to which he had so long
looked forward; the day on which he should know
the shouts and acclamations, the fine excitement of
new power.

Instead he took his command against hostility;
against dark faces and angry mutterings that his
foolish wilfulness over the old man had brought disaster on them all, even to their Sea King's death. In
all but seamanship they turned from him and looked

52

instead to the older Ragnar, who stood for Beorn, their dead leader's son. Helge seethed with rage and disappointment. The wearing heat had grown no less and the weight of his sweat-matted hair over his aching wound did nothing to ease his bitterness. He searched his angry and resentful mind to find a scapegoat, and fell immediately upon Ness.

From the moment of her capture she had been a thorn in his side. He too had wanted to take slaves on this raid to add pride and dignity to his following. But Anlaf had forbidden it, saying that they sailed light and he did not wish to feed them. Beorn alone was allowed this red-haired child. "She is but a child to keep him company," the Sea King had said easily when Helge protested.

Now in the ferment of his bitterness she seemed to him to be the source of all his disappointments and certainly a source of trouble in her wild talking of the vengeance of her God. In a rush of rage he leapt into the well deck, grabbing the startled child, and shaking her as his hound might shake a rat.

"I will tell you the cause of all the evil in this ship!" he yelled at the men. "Who knew of all the hermit's curses before they ever fell? Who told you of them? By the sword of Odin, she is more accursed than the old one himself! I will throw her to the sea, lest worse befall us."

Ness struggled helplessly in Helge's iron fingers, but before he could drag her to the side of the boat a furious Beorn was suddenly between them, wrenching her away from his cousin with a force that crashed her to the deck.

"She is *mine!*" he shouted. "*Mine!* And if she is the most evil thing on earth—and I think not—you cannot touch her. I am the Sea King's son; when we make landfall in our own country I am your chief, remember this, unless our people deny me. You are but my father's stern man until I am old enough to *show* myself his son and rule his fleet. Stay with your ships and leave what is mine alone! By the spirit of my dead father, I shall allow none to take his place until I do!"

Cheers and shouts arose for Beorn which Helge had expected for himself, and as his fair strong face darkened with fury, his ready hand flew to his sword. The boy did not move. Half the height of the young warrior, he stood before him eye to eye, beltless, unarmed even with his knife. The oars faltered and deadly silence fell upon the ship. The men inched closer towards Beorn; Ness still crouched where she had fallen. The long second seemed endless in the silence and the heat, and then Helge's sword hissed back into its scabbard as he found wisdom and turned away.

Ness got up slowly. "He will kill me secretly if he gets the chance. I do not understand, except that he hates me and I am afraid of him."

The boy threw her a glance. "He will kill me any way he can, and I am not afraid."

The girl turned away and wandered back between

the labouring rowers to throw herself wearily on the stern decking, as far away as she could get from Helge. She was very tired, exhausted by the long night of watching for the Sea King's death and shaken by Helge's threats. She watched the long row of dark Viking faces as they bent and stretched above their oars. In so short a time they had come far from the vital, roistering men who had come to raid her father's home. Now their sweat-streaked faces were drawn and weary, and in spite of the men who gave the stroke, their rowing had grown slow and ragged.

Beside Ness on the deck one of them had thrown down his tunic. Suddenly it lifted and fell, lifted again. For a few moments the girl stared at it without understanding and then she was on her feet, shouting wildly.

"Beorn! Beorn! It is the wind!" Whatever the strange heathen land might bring her, it was better to get there than to suffer this weight of heat and thirst. "The wind has come!" she cried again.

She had no need to shout. The cool breath had whispered all the way along the rows of tired faces until it lifted the hair on Helge's aching head where he stood on the foredeck, whipping the boat to new life and blowing aside all differences. Now they turned to Helge as the finest sailor in the fleet.

He stared to the west from where the wind came in fitful puffs, but his face was doubtful and for some time he would not order them to hoist the sail. Then the wind steadied and blew strong and cool and, for the first time since the island raid, the huge sail of white and scarlet billowed above the *Great Serpent* as she rode before the wind and the cheerful rowers eased themselves in their seats and pulled on their tunics against the cool welcome air.

But Helge turned his still-considering face to the west, where later in the day a dark bank of cloud began to creep up the blue sky like a stain. Gradually their steady wind grew fitful until it began to rush at the *Great Serpent* from all quarters, rising in great gusts to send the square sail swinging and thrashing, pulling the man at the stern oar from his feet as he wrestled to keep the ship before the wind.

"The sail!" yelled Helge. "Take down the sail! You will tear her to pieces!" The striped linen wavered down to the deck. The tall mast which in a storm could shake the loosebuilt longship into fragments was shipped to safety and the long black cloud raced up the sky while the breeze steadied again to a strengthening wind from its dark depths.

As the wind rose steadily, Ness watched with fear-wide eyes. The Vikings rushed to stow everything they could move below the decks and to close all the carved shutters when the oars had been shipped against the rising storm. They drew long lines below the keel of the boat and fastened them securely across the deck to give her timbers strength against the sea.

"You will be blown away!" yelled Beorn as he passed her. "Get to the well and hold on."

Bent double against the screaming wind, she did as she was told, stumbling and crashing from side to side against the thwarts until she tumbled, battered, into the shelter of the well deck. Here she was a little sheltered from the force of the gale, and she looked up to see the dark cloud creeping over their heads, blackening the blue sky and loosing sheets of rain that in a few moments ran from their hair and faces like the sea itself. Ness licked her lips and the salt was sharp on her tongue.

On every side of the rolling, tossing *Great Serpent* the waves rose now like dark mountains that collapsed endlessly in snarls of torn green foam; another rising in the same place to be torn to pieces in turn by the screaming wind. Only occasionally did Ness see Helge. Now and again when the driving rain was torn apart by the wind she saw him on the foredeck, his fair hair plastered to his head, water streaming from his clothes; or battering his way, bent double, round his tortured ship, lending his great strength at the steering oar where the mightiest of the Vikings were tossed about like puppets on a string.

Then through the darkness and the rain he was suddenly beside her, looking down at her where she crouched against a strake. There was no one near, only Helge, a great wet giant running with rain and sea, his eyes wide with pleasure at the chance he saw.

Ness opened her mouth, but no sound would come from her thick throat, and with one quick movement Helge scooped her up and flung her over the side of the heaving ship.

Now she screamed, in the second before the black water took her, but in the riot of the storm it was a hopeless whisper.

The sea rushed into her ears, her nose, and her open mouth, filling her head with a dark roaring and pressing her down, down, down to the depths of the great waves where death was waiting. Dimly she felt herself lifted again, rising up through the roaring water as strongly and fiercely as she had been dragged down. Faintly, far away, she thought her body crashed against hardness, and the water rushed away.

"I am dead," she thought.

"Bail!" yelled a voice. "Bail or die! Here, take this! Get up and bail, I tell you!" Beorn was shaking her violently.

She gathered her battered wits and looked about her; the sea itself must have saved her from Helge, throwing her back across the side of the *Great Serpent* even as he had thrown her over. The storm still raged, the mountainous seas towering over the ship.

Through the torn sheets of rain she could see the seas come pouring over the *Great Serpent's* stern, crashing over the men lashed to the stern oar, burying them in torrents of green water and tattered spray. Through the body of the ship the men bailed frantically with leather buckets, tubs, bowls, anything that came to hand in the struggle to relieve the poor wallowing *Great Serpent* of the weight of water which might in the end drag her down.

Then she remembered Helge. Frantically, she closed her numb fingers round the bowl which Beorn had given her and stumbled as fast as she could into the bailing well, thrusting to get close to the boy where she might know a small measure of safety. She clung as best she could with one hand and, bruised and battered already from her battle with the sea, she bailed wildly with the other, tossing out her pitiful small bowls of the great green seas which filled the *Great Serpent.* Sodden and sore, she had no eyes or mind for anything but the strake to which she clung and the small bowl with which she struggled against the ever-rising water at her feet. Once she saw dimly through her hazy mind the face of Helge, staring at her with surprise and fury, but she was now past fear.

She did not notice when the false dusk of the storm began to give way to the real dusk of the passing day. She paid no heed when Helge crashed along the boat's length, shouting frantic orders, nor noticed that the shutters were being drawn back and the Vikings were thrusting their oars once more into the boiling sea.

Still she bailed and clung, seeing nothing, until a cracking jar threw her off her feet. She crashed against the decking to the noise of splintering timber and the wild lurching of the ship veering in all directions. Sinking down into the swimming darkness which overwhelmed her, she felt the last fatal jar that shook the *Great Serpent* from its proud head down to the last whorl of its carved and gilded tail.

CHAPTER FIVE

NESS WOKE TO a cool wind and steadiness beneath her, but when she moved she could see nothing for the whirling of her head. She sensed Beorn beside her.

"What happened?" she said, pressing her hands to her head to try and steady it. "What happened? Did we not sink? Where are we?"

Slowly her head cleared and she sat up and blinked stupidly at Beorn, then she stared dazedly round her at the curved beach of fine white sand which stretched away from them, ending in a jagged headland from which long wicked rocks scattered out into the sea. High on the shore was the Great Serpent, tilted on her side, battered almost to a heap of timbers. Farther along the beach were three more of the longships, battered also, but none smashed as badly as the Great Serpent.

"Where are we?" Ness asked again. "What has happened to us?"

"We saw this bay through the storm and made for shelter. As we tried to pass the headland, we were caught upon the rocks. We were lucky then to be washed ashore. The other ships came later when the force of the storm was spent and they got in safely."

Ness looked at him. Her head was still thick and stupid and she could not think well, but she felt there was something wrong. The storm was a further disaster on top of all that had befallen, but there were three ships left; they were not stranded. There must be something else to account for the black anger in his face, it did not seem to be directed at her. The girl felt a pang of sorrow for him. Poor boy, his struggles with Helge had started so instantly on his father's death that there had been little time to grieve.

"What else is wrong?" She spoke with unaccustomed gentleness. "Why are you so angry?"

As always when he gave her his confidence, he spoke as though against his will. "Because," he burst out, "Helge wishes to bury my father in a broken ship, and without sacrifice. He says we cannot spare a ship, and there is no time to search this island for animals. Myself, I would like to sacrifice Helge in person," he added childishly and bitterly. "He wishes to bury my father in the broken Great Serpent— how can he travel safely to the other world in a broken ship? How can he make his journey? We have little enough to give him of what he ought to take, on account of all we have lost in the storm. And without sacrifice, how will the gods look kindly on him? Helge wants to bury him quickly and make all speed before this wind for home. He does not care if my father's spirit wanders restless for ever in

Q. What is anrwise?

the shades of Hel; all he cares is that he is dead—
and he can now try to seize all that was his!"

His voice was loud with anger and an anxiety
that Ness did not quite understand. She tried to
force her aching head to sort out all this talk of
sacrifices and broken ships as she rubbed tenderly
at the large bruise that had risen on the back of it.
Sorry for the boy, she tried to think with sympathy
of his pagan ways even if they horrified her, and to
understand that they meant much to him. This was
no time to try and tell him they were wrong.

Still dizzy and feeble she turned to him. "Well,"
she said, "what can we do?"

She should have known that for Beorn there would
be no thought without action. He jumped up and
seized her by the wrist, dragging her to her feet as
she tried to steady the tilting shore and the blue sky
that swung about her head.

"You will come," he said. "We will see what we
can do. Helge says this is an island. We will see how
big and what it holds; he would not dare to sail
without me."

Ness's gentle feeling towards him vanished. "I
am hungry," she protested mutinously. "And my head
hurts!"

A quick rush to the nearest group of men around
a fire and he thrust a lump of hot bread into her
hands.

"Now come, before Helge sees us. He is sleeping.
Your head will get better on the way!"

The land rose fairly swiftly behind the beach to small uneven hills, outcropped with rock and grown sparsely with a few stunted bushes and the occasional bent, wind-twisted tree. Through the rough stony grass behind the shore and up the lower slopes of the hills, Beorn pushed and stumbled at a rough determined trot, his brown face set, indifferent to anything that got in his way. Behind him, the dizzy and exhausted Ness scrambled on as best she could, her rage and irritation at this wilful boy rising with every step. If she stopped or fell behind, he turned and pulled her after him so roughly that it was easier to come herself. Only when they were immediately below the crest of the hill did he stop, sinking into a small hollow between two rocks.

Ness's breath whistled in and out of her dry throat. "Please do not stop for me," she gasped spitefully, but Beorn took no heed of her malice.

"It is folly to go swiftly over the top of a hill that you do not know. There may be an enemy immediately on the other side. Sit a moment and rest."

More furious because she had, as always, failed to anger him, the girl sank rebelliously down by his side, and looked back down the hill.

In the scene below, the darkness and fury of the storm seemed like a distant nightmare, brought to mind only by the helpless wreck of the collapsed and tilted Great Serpent. Now a fair wind blew from the west and high clouds drifted in a perfect sky, trailing their shadows over a glittering dark-green sea which lapped between the rocks on small secret beaches. In the distance lay other islands, pale and insubstantial, hovering fragile on the dark seas as if they might, in a moment, vanish. The shining air was sharp and fresh, tangy with a strange exhilarating smell. Ness took great gulps of it, feeling it clear her aching head and looking with pleasure on this strange and brilliant sea.

"Now we will go on," said Beorn, and sourly Ness turned to follow. In a few moments they lay down side by side and peered over the rocky crest.

There was a long silence and then Beorn gave a happy sigh. "Sacrifice and food," he said contentedly. "And I see streams for water. We are safe, but there shall be no raid. I shall insist on that; we have all we can do to get ourselves home."

Ness was silent, staring dumbly at what might be her last chance to escape before the longships finally left for their strange land in the north. Below them the hill sloped gently towards the south to where the sea ran through a sound between the island and a larger mass of land. On the grassy shores of the green water stood a monastery, many of its buildings made of mud and wattle crowned with the browning thatch of reed. Proudly in the centre, the oratory was raised in stone.

"It might be the one my father planned to raid," said Beorn.

Ness looked at the fields around the buildings, littered with the blackened traces of old foundations, half sunk into the lush green grass and softened with the spikes of pink and yellow flowers. "It seems to me that your friends have been here already." But she spoke without bitterness, looking thoughtfully round her at the islands and the monastery. "Where are we, do you know?"

"Helge knows these waters. He says that we are off the west coast of Scotia. Why?"

Wonder and delight shone in Ness's face. "Then I think I know where we are."

"Where?" The blue eyes were curious. Something in Ness's look held the boy's attention.

"We are on Iona. I am sure. The Holy Island, one of the holiest places in the world. The island of Columcille." She put out a hand and rubbed it gently on the rock beside her, her face still soft with awe and pleasure. Then she looked at the boy as though he surely, too, must understand. "You remember," she said urgently, "I told you of the warrior Columcille who became a priest. I am sure this is where he came. See, the day could not be more clear, but there is no sight of Ireland." She gazed back into the milky distance and the light left her face. "Poor Columcille," she said.

Beorn moved impatiently and peered again over the top of the hill. "Is this his monastery?"

Ness could not tell if he were interested, or merely trying to count the odds if he should meet a warrior priest. Now her voice grew bitter and she sank down well below the hill and stared back towards Ireland.

"You need not fear, he came three hundred years ago. These blackened stumps of ruins may well have been his buildings. He was so strong, they said, that for his oratory he raised the great stones single-handed, one upon the other."

Beorn had slipped down beside her, his restless fingers picking at the grass.

She did not look at him. "And yet so gentle," she went on, "and his voice so sweet, that when he sang the hymns he had made, the angels of God themselves stood up to listen."

"Angels? Ah yes, I have heard Macha tell. Valkyrie!"

Now it was Ness who looked puzzled, but she had lost his fleeting interest. Gentleness meant nothing to a Viking, and Beorn had turned to peer again over the hill. "You must be rested enough by now. Look, that is what I want!"

Close below them on the rocky hill, a cow moved slowly over the sparse grass, her calf nuzzling at her side. Ness joined him, but her mind was on the monastery and how she might attract the attention of the monks. For one wild moment she thought of running screaming down the hill, certain to attract attention, but cold sense washed over her. No use to shout at any stage. The long knife hung at the boy's belt and she was quite certain that were he in danger she would die first. She eased back a bit and tried to keep him talking in order to give herself time to make a plan; to give time in which someone might come out and walk about round that silent and seemingly empty monastery.

"Why," she asked, "do you always have to have a sacrifice? Is it not enough to pray for your father? Why must there be blood?"

Beorn looked at her. "It is only your women's God who would have prayers without sacrifice. Just women and old men talking!"

Now she was stung to answer him. "But of course we have sacrifice! Our God sacrificed His own Son."

Beorn, his blue eyes wide, slid down to face her close. "Your God did what?"

"He sacrificed His own Son." She was delighted but a little puzzled by the impression she had made. Beorn shook his head from side to side in admiration.

"That was indeed the bravest Viking thing to do! I have heard of it. Great Kings have done it when there was much at stake! What did your God want when he did this thing?"

Ness scrabbled wildly for words, almost exploding with laughter. Laugh she knew she must not. Brother Feredach had done nothing to prepare her for this. He had never thought of our Lord as a Viking.

"He wanted nothing for Himself," she said carefully. "He gave His Son for all Christians to open the way to Heaven. Every time the priest says Mass we offer up the sacrifice again."

The boy's eyes grew even wider, his face more

deeply impressed. "They offer up a man each time? This I did not know. This Macha never told us. Human sacrifice for us is only for the gravest reasons in the great temple at the Halls of the King!"

"Oh, no! No!" Ness floundered on wildly. "No, we present the sacrifice again when we say Mass and offer it up in bread and wine. Our Lord was only crucified once."

"Crucified?"

"Yes—He let himself be crucified for all of us. Was not that a great sacrifice?"

"Yes, indeed. I will say honestly, it was a Viking thing to do. Macha has told me some of these things but I did not listen." Suddenly his absorbed face cleared and with one of his sudden gestures he slid to the crest of the hill. "Come, we are wasting time. I want my sacrifice for my father."

Ness followed him and sighed as she looked over. There was still no one in sight, and nothing to do but go with him.

They moved in quietly among the cattle, who did no more than lift their heads in idle interest. All the time Ness kept one eye in desperate hope upon the monastery.

"This is easy," the boy unbuckled the leather belt round his waist. "I will take the calf and the cow will follow. You round up a couple more and drive them after her."

Ness watched the monastery and prayed as she

had never prayed before. It stayed still and silent and she began to think it was deserted.

"Here," said Beorn. "Take this and keep it ready. We may need it."

His eyes on the cow and her calf, he slipped the scabbard off his belt and handed it to the astonished Ness.

She stared at him. In his excitement and satisfaction, he had not thought to whom he was handing the knife. She stared at the fields between her and the monastery. One stroke and she could race across the grass to freedom; to the good monks of her own faith who would surely find a way to get her back to Ireland. She followed the boy as he carefully moved close to the unsuspecting cow and bent to fasten his belt around the calf's neck.

Her eyes grew wide. She saw the boy's back before her, his linen tunic strained across his strong young shoulders, and quietly she slid the knife out of the scabbard. The sweet heat of vengeance rushed into her brain; vengeance for her dead family; vengeance for the monks who had gone hurtling to their deaths while the Vikings laughed; vengeance for the poor old hermit, taken for a moment's sport and now left to his lonely death; vengeance for herself for all the pride and arrogance of this hateful Black Stranger. And freedom.

One more quick glance at the monastery, and her eyes glittered as the knife swung up to plunge itself into the grey linen and the boy's back.

"That will do well," said Beorn. He turned from the calf to find her as she had stayed, hand upraised, unable in the final moment to strike.

He looked from the lifted knife into her face. "Why did you not do it?" he asked her quietly.

The small soft calf rubbed against her legs and the mother lowed anxiously. Ness stared desperately into the boy's brown face, searching for a reason; searching deep in those strange dark-blue eyes, so large and long-lashed for a boy.

"I do not know! I do not know!" she cried in anguish. "I wanted to kill you!" Her hand fell slowly to her side and tears of confusion and disappointment filled her eyes.

Beorn took the knife from her limp fingers and smiled at her, for once without mockery.

"You are but a girl," he said, and then his voice grew a little curious. "Or maybe your gentle God would not let you?" The eyes sparked again. "Or maybe you begin to grow proud at last that you belong to me."

Ness was too confused to be angry. She had had the chance in one moment to dispose of her enemy and gain her freedom, and she had not been able to take it. She did not know whether she had lacked the courage for revenge or whether she had been given the grace to resist the temptation to kill. Humbled and a little ridiculous, she now did exactly as she was bid without protest. This was the dangerous part of the venture as they could not persuade the cattle to slip from rock to rock on the slope of the hill as they had done themselves. There remained, however, no sign of life about the wattle buildings.

"No doubt they are busy at their prayers," said Beorn, as he led the calf away, followed by its softly protesting mother. Ness took one last glance at her hopes of freedom and then followed after, plodding steadily behind the cattle until, in the late morning, the strange little procession arrived back on the shore where the Vikings were camped.

"See!" yelled Beorn, leaping on to a big rock as the men crowded around them. "See! I have brought you food and I have brought my father a sacrifice! Will you not now give him a whole ship that he may make his journey safely to the other world! It is his right and we are now very few. We can sail home in two ships. Will you give my father's spirit safety? Are you my men?"

His excited eyes blazed down on the Vikings below him. Standing up there in his tattered tunic, his hand still grasping the belt which held the calf, he looked strong and brave and wild and he was his father's son. Forgotten was the fact that Helge had brought them through the storm; that to him at this moment they owed their very lives.

"He shall have his ship!" they shouted.

"It is the chieftain's right!"

Beorn's face lit up with delight but, on the edges of the crowd, Ness watched Helge's thunderous face and felt a sharp quiver of fear for the boy whom she herself so recently had wished to kill.

That evening, as the luminous western twilight faded over the islands, Beorn entered fully into his place as Anlaf's son. One of the three sound ships was made ready for launching at the sea's edge and Anlaf's tent erected in the well. Into this were put all the belongings of the Sea King which had been saved in the Great Serpent's wreck. Ness watched from a little distance as they laid Anlaf carefully on his own bed, dressed with the rich coverings that were not often taken from their chests on an ordinary voyage. Around him they placed his arms, his drinking-horns, his bowls and cooking-pots, and all that they could spare of the seafaring tools which had been his life.

"It is a poor lot!" cried Beorn in anguish. "Had he been buried in our own land we could have sent great riches with him. He is ill equipped for so great a chief."

Ragnar soothed him. "We cannot do better. We never know how long it may take us to reach home, and we must not leave your father's spirit wandering." He bent as he spoke and placed a small piece of gold between the dead man's lips.

"Why do you do that?"

"I am an old man," answered Ragnar, "and this is an old custom. He may need it to pay whoever guides him across the dark water in his boat. We will bury him in the old way also, as the men have neither tools nor strength at the moment to raise a burial mound."

Beorn was still dissatisfied but the older man coaxed him away. "Come," he said. "As your father's son, it is your place to make the sacrifice. You come early to your duties."

Ness listened and her eyes were wide. Was it possible that Beorn should take a priestly rank, simply because he was his father's son? She thought of the monks in the abbey on the lake, gentle and humble, vowed to poverty, coming willingly in times of want or sickness to the poorest hovels on the islands. To these people here, priesthood seemed but another rank to add to the pride of those already mighty. No wonder the boy could not understand how a noble-man like Columcille could so humble himself in God's service.

Fires glittered along the shore in the lambent dusk; flames rose blue and green from salt-soaked wood, and near the funeral ship, a large rock had been moved into place as an altar. Small among the crowd-ing warriors, Beorn stood before it in the coloured firelight, and Ness watched, shocked and fascinated by the pagan rites. The two sacrificial animals were led up to him and she blessed herself and hid her face as the warm blood rushed from the still writh-ing carcass into the bowl in the boy's hands. She heard his voice lifted in incantation to his strange gods, begging for the safety of his father's spirit; heard the deeper echo of the answering Vikings and saw the blood spatter from Beorn's hands on to his father's body and the ship which would take it on its last dark journey.

Now the boy stood back and the men moved to lay their shoulders to the hull, easing the ship through the soft white sand and into the shallow water from where she would float away on the outgoing tide. Beorn held a blazing torch and, for one moment of hissing firelit silence, he paused before he raised his arm and flung the brand into the slowly drifting craft. Briefly, it lay burning on the deck and then seized greedily on the pitch-smeared timber, licking along the decking to catch the gunwales until the narrow boat was lined with fire, burning scarlet from the pitch, and laced with the sharp, clear, blue-green flames of salt. The tent blazed at last in the centre of the pyre, and on the shore the sacrificial meat was distributed to be cooked and eaten.

Out on the fire-streaked purple sea the flames took final hold on the drifting ship, a shivering pillar in the quiet dusk, until nothing remained but a livid skeleton on the darkening water, which moved gently seaward as the funeral feast was eaten on the shore.

At last Ness slowly took her shaking hands from her face, dazed with the strange wild drama of the bloody sacrifice, the burning ship and the rising merriment of the funeral feast along the firelit beach. She looked with pity at the solitary figure of the boy, alone now at the water's edge, and then gazed out across the widening distance at the drifting ship which took away for ever the body of Anlaf from those who had cared for him.

She whispered after him the prayer of her Church, offering it in her loneliness like a stick against the tide of these pagan rites. "*Requiam aeternam,*" she begged, "*dona eis Domine.*" Oh Lord, give him eternal rest. She spoke in Latin, as she had been taught to speak her prayers.

But down beside the sea, Beorn had no need for her pity. He stood where the water lapped unheeded round his feet and stared after the burning longship. His father, the Sea King, had gone on his last voyage with all possible honour according to his demands and the boy, his grief for the moment forgotten, swelled with pride and satisfaction. Helge should know who was chief.

Yet when at dawn of the next day the Vikings sailed for home in their two crowded ships it was Helge who stood in command on the foredeck, and Beorn, a disconsolate boy, who amused himself as best he could in the company of his Irish slave.

CHAPTER SIX

GETTING OVER HER first grief and loneliness, Ness felt her spirits beginning to rise in the bright air of Beorn's windswept country. The falling golden leaves carpeted the great beech forests behind his homestead, and to the front of it long sandy spits ran down into the glittering sea. The ceaseless wind raked her long hair and her eyes were hungry for the mountains in this land so flat that when she first saw it from the tossing longship, it looked no more than a line drawn between sea and sky. The air was clear and brilliant and in the late sunlight the grass shone rich between the feet of the browsing cattle. The skies seemed wider and more full of light than she had ever seen them in her soft damp homeland.

She had been met with tears and affection by Macha, the Irishwoman, who grieved deeply for Anlaf but was delighted to have a child of her own country and her own Christian faith to keep her company. Macha had risen until she cared for the whole of the chief's household and Ness was to live with her in the warm women's room which lay partly underground so that it would be comfortable against the winter's cold. Macha showed her her own spot where she could sleep on the wide bench which ran all round the walls, cushioned for a sitting place by day, and at night a bed for everybody.

Ness had looked curiously at this arrangement, and at all the others so different from what she was accustomed to and, especially, she had gazed in wonder at the Great Hall of the Sea King. She compared it with that of her uncle who was an under king at home. Here the fire was not square in the middle of the floor; it ran long and narrow down the length of the Hall, raised from the floor on a platform of stones. There were steps all the way along the sides of the immense room, wide enough to hold chairs along the top one and trestle tables along the second when it was time to eat. The lowest step close to the fire was spread with rugs and cushions so that people coming from the cold might sit and warm themselves. Presiding over all was the huge chair set in the middle of the long wall, flanked with carved pillars reaching to the smoky roof. This, Beorn told her, was the high chair of the chief.

"And where do they sleep?" she asked him. "By the fire?"

"For the family and the upper servants there is another sleeping hall apart. The thralls sleep here around the fire."

She gradually discovered the size of the big household; the kitchen; the pantry; the storehouse; the guest hall; the bath-house. From Macha she learnt her duties in the immense task of caring for it all.

It seemed to be forgotten that she was supposed to be the property of Beorn and she settled as happily as was possible into her new life among the women. It was a life in which she saw very little of the boy and even though his arrogance still drove her into fury, she was willing to admit secretly that she missed his company. She was also touched that in spite of all the talk that she was his, the iron collar of the thrall was not forged around her neck and she walked free as Macha.

He would come sometimes, as he had done from childhood, into the warm kitchen in the evenings before the late meal. He sat toasting himself on the bench close to the kitchen fire, full of his day's doings, teasing Macha and picking at her cooking until she slapped his hands away and told him to be gone. Often then he would turn to Ness, snatching at her tunic as she passed him, telling her to sit down and let him have some more tales of her gentle God and His warrior priests. In the red glow of the fire his dark face was half derisive and half curious.

When he wanted to talk of these things Macha would push Ness from the cooking and whisper to her to sit beside him and tell him all she could. In all her captive years Macha had never forgotten that she was a Christian. She had passed on her faith to several of the Viking women and it was her dearest wish to give it to Beorn, who was the treasure of her

heart. But through his childhood years he had only laughed at all her talk of God. Now, she saw, he would listen to Ness, and ask for more.

So in the lengthening autumn evenings, while the savoury pots hissed and bubbled on the fire, Ness breathed a prayer for help to Brother Feredach and tried to tell the great truths of her faith.

She told him of the first Christmas and the coming of the Baby in the stable, while the star blazed in the East and the angels sang above the cowering shepherds on the frosty hill.

Beorn banged his bare brown knees and shouted with laughter, to think that a King should come so low and still hope to keep his subjects.

"But He has," Ness said, offended. "That was eight hundred years ago, and He is still our King. Can you tell me a Viking chief who has reigned eight hundred years?"

Beorn looked at her and was silent and Macha smiled above her pots.

She told him of the first Easter, when the Romans raised the Cross outside Jerusalem and crucified our Lord; and the darkness fell across the earth. This was language he could understand; blood and death and sacrifice. But the reason for it he could never follow.

"Why? Why? Why did He do it? Why should so great a King humble Himself? It makes no sense. When I am chieftain, I will be proud, *proud.* I will hold my people by my pride and strength of arms as I grow to be a man. These are the things! Your God is too gentle! I hold still to ours, they are the gods for a *man!*"

Macha shook her head.

But outside the warm kitchen Beorn was fighting with everything save weapons for his position in his father's house. When they had first returned and the battered longships had grounded at last on the sands below his home, Beorn had firmly taken his place on his father's high seat between the carved pillars of the gods. Scowling bitterly, Helge had given in with ill grace and taken his seat opposite him in second place.

Equally Beorn had taken his father's place when

the great sacrificial feast was held in the temple to give thanks for their safe homecoming, and to drink the wine to the memory of all those who had not returned. But when the warriors of the household were mustered outside the barrack halls below the outer wall it was Helge who stood in command. Bright-haired and vigorous under the weight of his huge weapons, it was he who trained them in all the arts of war. In the fierce sports with which the Vikings loved to develop their mighty strength he was always the winner. It was always Helge who, fully armed, could run fastest, leap longest and jump from the greatest height; Helge, bright with confidence and strength, who could walk with all his weight of arms along the oar of the moving longship.

Beorn was apart with the other boys, only now learning all these things from Ragnar. He was fiercely jealous of the skill and strength of Helge and the way his warrior's prowess was slowly winning back his popularity with the men.

"I do not understand," Ness said on one of these evenings when Beorn joined her at the kitchen fire. "Why does Helge not simply kill you now, and be done with it? The men are his again and I think you are in great danger."

"It is not quite as easy as that for him," answered the boy, holding out his hands to the blaze. His cheeks were flushed and his dark eyes clear and bright from his long day in the open. "These warriors here are only a handful. There are far, far more

Why didn't he kill him

in the scattered homesteads of my father's province. These are the landowners who must vote as to who shall be the chief at the next parliament; probably in the spring. Until then, we cannot really know whose man is whose, although Ragnar has a fair idea who is mine. Helge dare not act before then or he may lose everything. In the spring he might get it all without a fight. But I doubt it," he added pompously, "for I am, after all, my father's son." Leaning back out of the firelight, Ness grinned across at Macha.

Ragnar did not have Beorn's faith that Helge would wait for the voting. He watched the boy ceaselessly, keeping him always at his side, and at night he locked them both into one of the little rooms at the end of the big sleeping chamber beside the Hall. When he slept himself, his sword was always at his hand.

"At least," thought Ness with relief, "it has taken Helge's mind away from me."

It was obvious that Helge himself did not find patience easy. His dark face and offensive manner towards the boy told that he would find it much simpler to use his sword.

Thus the tense and divided household passed the golden days of late autumn, when the last of the falling leaves left the beechwoods stark and grey and the wide skies were filled with the empty honking of the south-bound geese. With the first frost, Macha fussed that it was time to open the great chests of furs and rugs to air them for the winter's use.

With the first frost, too, came Helge's visitors; tall and broad and fair as he himself, arrogantly straddling their pale high-necked northern horses, and sweeping into the paved court with a clatter of hoofbeats and a clash of arms that brought the household running anxious to the doorways.

The white-clad thralls ran to lead away the horses and Helge was summoned from the school of arms. He arrived in haste to fall upon the neck of the tallest stranger. He shouted his pleasure and led them all into the Hall in a flurry of cold air, the warm, sweaty smell of horses and the clatter of discarded arms.

Beorn did not see them until evening. Hunting all day in the forests, he came back gratefully through the frosty dusk to where the firelight glowed red and welcoming behind the skin windows of his Hall. He stepped inside the door and threw down his spears, staring in surprise at his unexpected guests. In the rich light of the long fire they sprawled along the cushions of the lowest bench, drinking-horns in their hands, their clothes loose and easy in the heat and their voices loud and over merry. In their midst sprawled Helge, warm and hospitable.

As Beorn came slowly down the long room, Helge got up, magnificent in the red light which flickered on his fresh-combed hair and beard and on the rich embroidery of the long buttoned coat that reached his feet. His face was bright with welcome and his hands outstretched.

"Ah, my cousin Beorn!" he cried. "In your absence

I presumed to make welcome these good friends from my own country. They have come in kindness to condole with me on your father's death. They knew I held him most dear. My kinsmen, my friends—this is my young cousin Beorn, who sits at the moment in his father's place as chief."

Helge's speech ended with a hiccup and a foolish giggle and Beorn looked in bewilderment from face to face. That they had all drunk far too well from his father's good ale was obvious. But what else? Another time, too much ale would have made Helge murderous. What was he up to that he should speak so civilly? What lay behind these fair words? He looked again at the strangers, turning from one fair rugged face to the next. They were all of them older than Helge and scarred with many battles. But even when they spoke as cordially as Helge himself, he read in each pair of eyes the same derision and contempt which he had heard in his cousin's voice. And over the faces of all their followers who stood behind them rippled the same amusement.

Beorn felt young and helpless and his scalp crept under his hair with a warning of danger that he sensed, but did not understand. For a long moment they stared at each other in the firelight; the huge fair men in their rich garments of leisure, and the short, dark boy, his clothes stained from his day of sport.

From the darkness at the back of the Hall, Ness watched him visibly stiffen and make himself taller, and her heart warmed to his pride that was not always foolish. Now it allowed him to hold his ground with dignity, bidding the strangers welcome to his house, thanking them for their kind words about his father.

"I presumed also, Cousin," went on the new, smiling Helge, "to order a feast to be prepared in their honour. Did I do right?"

"You did right."

Beorn's voice was short, and he noticed as he left the Hall that the feast in preparation seemed to be one for the most noble of guests. The straw of everyday was being brushed from the floor and his father's most precious skins and carpets from the east had been laid in its place. On the highest step, the long row of carved chairs had been heaped with rich cushions and draped with furs. Along the tables set up in front of them, Ness moved with the best of silver plates and the drinking-horns, carved and gilded and bound in ivory, which had been his father's pride.

"He makes too free with these treasures that are not his own," the boy hissed to Ragnar as they went out. "And with my father's ale. My ale. Who are these men that they must be feasted with the best we have to offer?"

"I only know the eldest," Ragnar answered thoughtfully. "He is a kinsman of Helge's from Scania. As for what they are here for, that I cannot guess. They do not care a fig for your father, any more than Helge does. But go easily, my son, and with care. Try to curb your temper, although it may be hard, and give fair words for fair until we can discover what they intend."

The Hall reeked of new-lit lamps when the boy went back, and the light fell clearer on all the sumptuous preparations for the feast. But he kept his calm face and moved steadily to his guests and bade them sit round him in his high seat. He had the satisfaction of seeing Helge compelled to take his place across the fire, only among the followers of his friends. He held firmly to his dignity in his place as chief, except when Ness came with Macha to bring food to the table, and then he turned from his guests to give her a secret, triumphant grin.

Helge's visitors remained a mystery. His own good humour increased with every day, and he made Beorn the object of a hilarious friendliness that was more insulting and infuriating than his previous surliness had ever been. There were long days when he and his friends were missing, supposedly on hunting trips. But the game they threw to Macha at the day's end was strangely little. One of the troop of housecarls that rode to attend them came to Ragnar. He told him that half the time they did not hunt. They rode deep into the forest or the heathland, and there in some sheltered spot talked endlessly, both the visitors and many of Helge's own warriors of the household company.

"Did you hear anything that was said?" Ragnar asked anxiously.

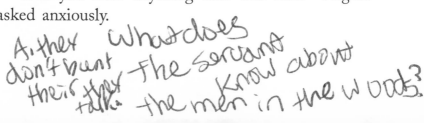

"No, no. Nothing. They keep us at a distance, my lord Helge jesting that they have much to talk about, having been so long apart."

Ragnar praised him for his information, bidding him watch and listen all he could. Like most of the servants, the man favoured Beorn, having known him since his birth. Later, after some thought, the older man told the boy what he had heard.

"What does it mean?" Beorn stared at Ragnar. He had a knife in one hand and in the other an arrow which he feathered. "What does it mean? If Helge wants my father's place, I do not see he needs these strangers to get it for him for he may get it in the spring with no effort. But certainly he plots some mischief. His good humour tells me this, if nothing else. My cousin has always been most charming in his words when his actions were most evil. I distrust and I *hate* him. Why can we not *act!*" A savage thrust of the knife sheared off half the arrow and the blade slipped down to the boy's hand, bright blood instantly beading the brown skin.

"That is why, my son," Ragnar smiled as Beorn flung the ruined arrow to the ground and angrily sucked his wound. "That is why—haste and thoughtlessness nearly always bring disaster. It is not enough to be brave, it is necessary to be wise also. Let us wait and watch a little longer and perhaps we may find out more."

Ness discovered Helge on another evening when she slipped across the chilly starlit courtyard to the byre. She loved the warm, rich-smelling stable which made her think of those at home, and she was anxious to see and pet a small new calf which had arrived that day. The door of the byre was a little open and Ness was ready to be angry with the careless thrall who had left it so, chilling the mother and her new-born calf on so cold a night. As she moved to slip through, she was halted by the sound of rough voices, talking urgently and low. She stopped at once and shifted the heavy door only a fraction so that she could peer round it.

A single torch was stuck in the middle of the earthen floor and a circle of men crouched talking in its warm, smoky light. Helge was there and his three friends and some of their followers. With them were a few of the leaders of the household company. Helge was talking fiercely, drawing as he spoke with a piece of stick on the floor, raising his face into the glow to explain what he had drawn, and drawing again irritably when they did not understand. Then one of the strangers seized the stick to draw and talk in his turn.

"If I could only hear and understand!" thought Ness. Beorn and Macha had both been teaching her, but her Danish was still slow and hesitant.

Carefully, she pressed the door to open it a little farther and the protesting wood leaned on its uneven hinge-pole and moaned loudly. Around the fire, the bearded heads flashed up and the men leapt to their feet. In the same instant, Ness vanished like a shadow round the corner of the byre. They came out at once, peering here and there in the wavering torchlight.

"Be *quiet!*" snarled Helge. "I tell you, it is nothing but the wind. Do not make an uproar so that we are noticed!"

"I *trust* it was the wind," said the tallest stranger. "But we are wise to be quiet. Go your ways, men, quickly—we will meet again."

As soon as they were gone, Ness fled for Beorn and together they took a torch and ran to examine the stable floor.

"If anyone comes we can say we have come to see the calf," Ness panted as they dropped on their knees where the men had crouched. But the floor had been scraped clean with a hasty shoe, all except one corner where a shape still showed in the dark earth.

"It looks like nothing," Ness mourned.

"It looks like one of my father's sea charts. Of the island of Seeland to the east. But I cannot see what that may mean if Helge seeks my father's lands." Beorn tilted his head this way and that over the drawing.

They told Ragnar, who could make nothing of it either, and through every day of friendliness and courtesy they watched and waited to see what treachery might lie behind it.

They waited until the day when Macha decided that the time had really come to open all the great carved chests and get out the woollen covers and the fur-lined rugs needed to cover the beds against the increasing cold and also the women's heavy woollen cloaks and the huge fur and sheepskin coats belonging to the men. Ness went to get them where Macha bade her, but came back so much later with her warm and heavy burden that Macha's long Irish face was creased with anger.

She scolded Ness. "Where have you been, lazy one? Did it take all this time to creep beneath the bekkir and lift the first rugs?"

Ness stared at her as if she did not hear, her eyes far away. "Where can I find Beorn? Or my lord Ragnar?" she asked at last.

"What of them? What of them? They will not be here until dusk. They have gone to search the forest for a bear that has been seen by the woodcutters. Now go again and bring me what I tell you *at once*."

Ness possessed herself as best she could in patience through the long day as she carried the heavy loads of furs and sheepskins and watched and turned them before the fire. The stars were pricking through the vast frosty sky when sounds of the returning hunters brought her flying to the courtyard.

"Quickly! Come with me. I must talk to you." She plucked at Beorn's sleeve, but he tossed her hand away.

"Another time. Another time. See, we have a bear to skin! And the spear that took him was mine. Ragnar says I may have him for my bed, and that is only right, as I am Beorn the Bear!"

Full of pride and excitement, he swaggered and

strutted round the huge carcass, preening himself in the praise of the servants who had crowded to admire it. Ness danced with irritation and her ill-heard message burned in her mind. In the end she turned to Ragnar, pulling at his sleeve to hold his attention.

"My lord Ragnar! I beg you to allow me speak with you. I have heard something which I think important and Beorn will not listen to me."

Ragnar did not brush her off. "He is excited and proud," he said. "It is his first bear, let him be. If you have something to tell, then let us walk in the shadows away from the light and the crowd, that we may hear but not be heard."

Beorn missed her and rushed after them. "Why did you go away?" he demanded. Ness threw him an exasperated glance. "I was just about to listen. What is it? What is it?"

"Quiet, my son, quiet! Helge has a thousand ears. Speak gently, girl, and tell us what it is."

Ness gathered her tangled thoughts. It had been a long day to carry a message in a language she had only just begun to understand and now she could not bring it out in order. "Today," she began slowly, "Macha bade me creep beneath the benches where the chairs stand in the Hall to get the winter rugs from the big chests that are stored there."

"What of that?" the boy began impatiently, but Ragnar stayed him.

"Go on," he said.

"I crept farther than the chests to see what it was

like, and when I was under the far end of the Hall, my lord Helge and his friends came in and sat above me and I overheard their talk."

She felt both her listeners stiffen and Ragnar glanced round quickly and edged her a little deeper into the shadows. She groped for the rest of the story, trying to repeat what they had said. It came out as a question.

"What did it mean when Helge said he would send out the arrow?"

Now Ragnar had her by both arms, his fingers deep in her flesh, and she felt Beorn draw so close that his breath was warm on her cheek.

"Where?" asked Ragnar hoarsely. "*Where* did Helge say he would send out the arrow?"

"It was hard," Ness protested. "I did not really understand, but I think he said he would do it here and his friends would do it in their own land. Does that make sense?"

"What else? What else?" Ragnar shook her as if he would shake the words out of her.

"I did not understand!" cried Ness again. "Something about marching while the water is hard, as he has no boats since the fleet was lost off Ireland. Please let go, you are hurting my arms!"

Ragnar did let her go, his face abstracted in the dim light. "March while the seas are frozen? Yes, but where? From Scania to here? He does not need that host to kill a boy."

Ness dredged to the bottom of her confused mind.

"Who," she asked slowly, "is Eyvind the Ancient? It is against him that they said they will march." She turned her head from side to side as she felt the man and the boy draw back with shock and then turn silently to meet each other's eyes.

Beorn faced back to her at last, as if he moved in his sleep. "Eyvind the Ancient," he said heavily, "is the King of all Denmark. What you have heard means that Helge will call out his host of Vikings here, and his kinsmen will do the same in Scania. While the seas are frozen they will march from two directions upon the island of Seeland and the Halls of the King. No wonder my cousin now feels I am only a jest."

CHAPTER SEVEN

FOR HOURS they discussed Helge's plan, locked secretly in the small sleeping room while one of the servants kept watch at the door of the long chamber.

"It is a strange time," said Beorn, "to make an attack. In the winter when the snow may be deep."

"Helge has, as he says, no ships to cross the water, there are only two left here. And I think perhaps there is haste lest the Ancient One should die and a stronger man take his place before the plan comes to fruition. Helge will be all right. It has been a fine summer and a good harvest. All the barns will be full on his way and the cattle fat."

"Is the King very old?" Ness asked.

"Near to a hundred years, but still, they say, fierce and wise."

"He will also think himself safe in the winter," mused Ragnar. "He will not expect attack. Now," he went on more vigorously, "now that we have at last learned Helge's plans, we must make our own."

"We must warn the King!" cried the boy.

"More than that. How long do you think you

would live if Helge found you had thwarted his ambitions? He would raze the Halls of Anlaf to the ground. No, all of us who support you, Beorn Anlafsson, must go. And we must go in such secrecy that Helge thinks we have run from him and from his power. He must never suspect that we have gone to the King."

[handwritten margin notes: Why do they call him Beorn Anlafsson.]

Beorn edged closer, excitement blazing in his blue eyes as Ragnar talked and laid his plans before them.

Ness, however, listened in dismay. "What of me? she cried to them as he finished. "What of me?" Do you leave me here that your cousin may spit me for his dinner! As he would without a thought."

Beorn looked uncertain. In his excitement, he had forgotten her.

"It will be no place for you," Ragnar said at once. "You have served us well, but you will be quite safe here. Helge has other things on his mind and will not notice you. In any case, he has never done any actual harm. He only threatens you."

"Oh, he only threatens! I will tell you!" Full of alarm at the idea of being left with Helge, Ness poured out the story of how he had flung her into the sea in the storm. The man and the boy both stared at her, Beorn in rising anger.

"Why did you not tell me this before?" he demanded.

"You were always so angry with Helge, anyway. I did not need to add anything else."

He glared at her a few moments longer, then, "You

will come with me," he said shortly, and whipped round on the protesting Ragnar. "Unless she comes I do not go."

The older man shrugged and raised his hands in hopelessness, but Ness smiled a small contented smile.

Now it was the turn of Beorn's followers to hold their secret meetings and their false hunting trips when, in the deep heart of the beech forest, Ragnar's picked men would gather in secrecy and excitement to discuss their plans. There was not a great deal of time. It was now drawing towards the feast of Yul and the dark northern days grew short and the frosts keener.

"We must make haste." Ragnar looked up at the vast night sky that blazed with frosty stars, while to the north the darkness glowed with soft flickering ribbons of coloured light. "The Fires of the Gods are glowing and the frost is hardening. If we are to get our ship across the land, we must waste no time or the inland waters will be frozen."

"What does he mean," Ness asked afterwards, "about getting the ship across the land?"

"We cannot wait," answered Beorn, "like Helge, until the seas are frozen. We must cross by water to the island of Seeland where lie the King's Halls. We will take the one longship that has been mended. She has been berthed for the winter, but my men have been working secretly these past days to get her ready for sea. As she is laid up, she will not be missed. And at this time of year we dare not sail round north Jutland where the two seas meet. It would also bring us too close to Scania and Helge's friends. So we will divide our people into two parties, so that Helge will not miss us all too quickly. The first party will sail south in the longship. We, the second party, will go by land down the Warrior's Road a night later, to the river Eider at the south of Jutland. Here we will meet the ship and here it is possible to take the boat across the neck of land. There are waterways, and where there is no water, the boats are carried."

"Carried?" Ness's mouth opened as she thought of the mighty longships.

"Longships are light. But we shall still need every man we have to carry it. Then we shall all sail to Seeland from the other side."

The girl thought of her earlier travels. She pulled a wry mouth and shivered.

"And with which party will I go?" she asked.

"You will come by land with me."

Ness grimaced at his departing back. But at least, she thought, he told me all his plans quite willingly. And so he ought, for did I not find out for him all my lord Helge was up to!

Macha was also to travel. Ragnar had gone to her to get her to pack secretly all the food that both parties would need for the journey and she had refused to be left behind.

"Alone with that villain!" she had cried. "Your pardon—alone with my lord Helge when he finds you have all escaped him. He would slit my throat and drink my blood for no more reason than that my lord Anlaf and his son have cared for me. No, I will come. By land, mark you, for I am no lover of your tossing longships, but I will come. I can cook for you and care for the two children, who are no charge for men. Now, there is no more talk, my lord Ragnar. It is all arranged. There will be others too, I do not doubt, who will prefer to come. We will be useful."

Beorn and Ness exchanged smiles as the greying Ragnar gave in like an obedient boy.

"We have always done as Macha says," said Beorn. "I think it is really she who ruled my father's house. I would not be surprised if, when we reach the Halls of the King, she does not take control there too!"

The day came when Helge announced the departure of his friends and, schooled by Ragnar, Beorn took his opportunity. Their guests from Scania must not go, he said, without a proper farewell. There should be the greatest hunt that they had ever seen and, on the following evening, Helge must permit him to give them a parting feast of suitable magnificence. They must not leave until after this, he would not hear of it.

Helge's mouth fell open into his blond beard and he stared at the boy in amazement; until now Beorn had offered his guests nothing but poor hospitality and worse manners.

"By all the gods, cousin, it's most kind of you," he gaped.

Ness turned away to hide a smile, but well she knew that it was no joke to Ragnar and the others who were working to get ready for the journey without arousing any suspicion in Helge or his followers. It was fortunate that they themselves were too deep in their own plans to notice anything odd in the behaviour of other people.

Ness watched the four fair giants pacing the wide courtyard, deep in conversation, "Tell me," she said quietly to Beorn, "is it Helge they will make king if they succeed? And why? Why should he be King more than any of the others; has he any right?"

"A small one. As big as need be if he carries enough arms. Long years there have been two kings of Denmark—sometimes only one when one was strong enough to defeat the other. The Ancient One has been so strong, and has been King alone for many years, ruling all Denmark from Seeland. Helge, they tell me, is kinsman near enough to the last king of Jutland whom the Ancient One defeated. And Helge is strong and brave and handsome and men follow him. That is enough." Beorn's eyes followed the girl's to the four tall figures and for a moment his face was dark and sombre. Then his eyes lit. "But now I have a chance. Should the King's host defeat Helge, my troubles are over and my father's Halls are mine." Then he began to laugh outright. "Now I must go and talk to Ragnar about this hunt that I am so kindly arranging for my favoured guests."

Across the court Helge shot a suspicious glance as

the boy's laugh rang out and the two children slipped away into the shadows.

It was Ragnar who arranged the hunt, choosing carefully those who were invited to ride upon it. Elk had been sighted, he said, in great numbers on the inland heath, and the day promised well. From the door of the warm kitchen the two children watched the hunters assemble in the sharp grey light of the frosty morning. On the stone flags of the court the fresh horses clacked and fretted with their restless hooves, tossing their high, arched necks and blowing out their breath to hang in warm clouds on the frosty air. The Vikings shouted and stamped and clapped their gloved hands, hair and beards flowing down over great sheepskin coats as pale as their horses' flanks, their weapons dulled by the stilling touch of the frost. Only their faces lived and glowed as they leaned from their saddles to grasp the last horns of warm ale. Rime stiffened the grass round the courtyard edge and stood in ridges on the trees, and the head of the *Great Serpent,* which Beorn had placed above the door, was sharply crowned in white.

"It is well that we are ready," whispered Beorn. "The frost hardens. Go give my poor lord Helge a warm drink—it may be long before he sees another!"

Ness tried to still her shaking shoulders and Beorn dug her in the ribs with his elbow, laughter and excitement spurting up in both of them.

"Quiet now," said Macha cautiously. "You will attract your cousin's notice."

But that did not stop them rushing into the kitchen as the huntsmen clattered out of the gates, and throwing themselves on the cushions of the benches, rolling with laughter until they had to stuff their tunics in their mouths to try and stop.

"Foolish things," said Macha tolerantly as she moved among her pots.

"We are only thinking of how much Helge and his friends will enjoy the hunt, and we are happy for them," said Beorn weakly as he wiped his eyes.

Helge and his friends hunted through the long bright day when the sun melted the rime to water and then dried it where it lay. On the inland heath the land stretched unending to the arching sky with here and there a small lake or an idling group of trees or a marshy, treacherous stretch of bog. Over these vast empty spaces the hunt thundered on their strong short-legged horses, searching for the herds of elk that had been seen first here, then there, then somewhere else, by the willing servants whom Ragnar had sent out to scout for them. The day lengthened and tempers shortened and unused weapons grew heavy in the hand as irritable eyes scoured the empty plains for elk or indeed for any game that would give a chase.

In the end the tireless Ragnar led them from the fruitless chase on the empty heathland. "There are bear and boars in the forest in plenty. We will make for them!" he cried. He wheeled his horse and hurtled for the dark shadows of the distant pinewood.

Game there was in plenty and the bags were quickly filled. Fierce with the joys of killing at the end of an empty day, the visitors failed to notice the deepening shadows that filled the forest as the short day ended. It was Helge who first drew rein, brushing his damp hair from his forehead under his sheepskin cap.

"Friend Ragnar," he said, "the night comes on."

Ragnar gazed around him in surprise as the rest of the hunt rode up, pale as great moths between the darkening trees. "Indeed," he said, amazed, "by the father of the gods, I did not notice in the heat of the chase. It grows dark!" He looked around him again and up at the first bright stars which spiked the top of the pine trees and once more a mild surprise lit his face. "I fear," he said regretfully, "we are *very* far from home."

Helge looked at him suspiciously, but Ragnar smiled in mild apology and signalled his huntsman to raise the long curved horn that would call the stragglers round them for the ride back.

Ragnar was thoughtful to see that none were missing before he would start. "It would be a poor finish to their visit should any of your men be left in strange country." He smiled kindly and helpfully at the now glowering visitors who fretted on their chilling horses as the bitter night wind plucked at their cheeks and thick darkness fell like a blanket on the forest. Through this they struggled home, crashing, cursing through the undergrowth and plodding slowly

over the endless heathland on their now exhausted horses. It was late into the night when they flung themselves at last from their saddles before the welcome light of the Hall. My lord Helge, as Beorn had foreseen, raised angry bellows for hot ale before ever his horse had stopped.

Long before this hour, the friends of Anlaf's son had gathered quietly in from the dark countryside. Ignored by Ragnar's carefully chosen guards, they met in the deep shadow of the huge boathouse. When they were all gathered, the vast doors opened silently from inside and the newly repaired longship, patchy with fresh timbers, slid down her rollers into the dark

water, moving as quietly as if she herself knew the
need for secrecy. Swiftly the men clambered on board,
and by the time the weary huntsmen plodded into
the courtyard, she was gliding like a shadow southwards over the icy sea.

All the huntsmen slept late the next day and when
Helge finally emerged into the Hall, he gazed at the
preparations for the feast with a sour and doubtful
eye. "By Thor's hammer, boy," he snarled at Beorn, "I
hope your feast is better than your hunt."

"Oh indeed, my cousin!" Beorn fought to hold his
twitching face. "I promise you it will be excellent. I
hear you had poor sport yesterday and that the foolish Ragnar led you far out of your way. It was bad—
and your friends, my guests! But never fear, tonight
will be different!"

Helge glowered and tugged at his tangled beard,
irritable and suspicious of he knew not what. But
Beorn smiled and left him, and when the feast took
place that evening there was nothing he could fault.

The hearth fire blazed high and brilliant down
the centre of the long room, adding its dancing
glow to the lamplight which fell over the laden
tables. Macha had brought out everything that could
do honour to the Halls of Anlaf, and the room
glowed with the brilliance of warm colour and embroidery, and the soft sheen of rich furs thrown
across the chairs and benches. Here and there in
horns and vessels, the firelight splintered on the
gleam of jewels and it glowed softly in the wide

silver hoops around the wine and the ale butts at the table ends.

From the women's table at the end, Ness looked down the two long rows of men. They sprawled before their piled plates and shouted to the servants as they passed with smoking pots. They pushed the food into their mouths with their knives or tore happily at long lengths of sausage. Ragnar had done his work well, and the best of ale and wine flowed freely. Tongues were loose and voices loud. Long endless tales of past victories drowned the voices of the skalds singing by the fire and left the leaping acrobats unheeded. Washing down the meat with great draughts of ale and wine, they called the gods to witness the truth of their boasting and, more than once, flushed, angry faces pushed close to each other over half drawn swords. Opposite Beorn sat Helge, delighted with the honour shown to his guests. His face was crimson against his blond disordered hair and his voice loud and boastful as he gestured wildly with a silver horn. Ness stole a secret glance at Beorn, a small satisfied smile, for they knew that Macha had put something into the last ale barrel that would give long, deep sleep to Helge and his friends that night.

"And why does my lord Ragnar not allow you to put in too much and kill him?" Ness had asked earlier as she watched Macha prepare the drink. "Helge is wicked—I do not see that the Vikings mind killing anybody, even the good."

"You become a heathen yourself among these people. Since when have we thought it right to kill? Besides," she went on more practically, "even if it were good to kill Helge, my lord villain, it would not be wise. He has too many friends. My boy Beorn would not last an hour."

As the wicks sank low into the lamps, so many of the Vikings slumped into their chairs before their tumbled plates and empty horns, and others stretched themselves before the fire. Helge's head fell slowly on his wine-stained chest and Beorn rose immediately from his high seat, followed by all his men, who had spent the evening plying their enemies with wine but drinking nothing themselves. Now they left the long Hall, stepping carefully over the snoring shapes around the fire, stooping here and there to drag a body over so that a careless hand or foot flung into the flames would not wake a sleeper too soon.

At the door Ragnar paused to look back. Those not already asleep were too drunk to notice anything and the hour was ripe. He and Beorn lifted the heavy outside door and dropped it firmly in its socket, fastening it securely on the outside. The night was drawing towards the morning and the still frost had given way to a biting wind that blew from the heart of the wavering glow that filled the northern sky. In the banquet Hall of Anlaf the fire died low, sinking towards the sacrilege of a cold hearth, and around it and above it on the carved and bolstered chairs, Helge and his followers sprawled in sleep.

The guards that night had also been Macha's trust, receiving gratefully the hot spiced drinks she brought them to keep out the cold of the icy wind. Now they sprawled asleep, lying as they fell, weapons all askew beside them, and Beorn and his companions stepped over them as they set out on their journey. Long before the guards, or the Vikings in the Hall, woke up to evil tempers and thick-tasting mouths, daylight was clear over the Warriors' Road, lifting the spirits and speeding the steps of the party who marched to the south, wrapped in their furs against the bitter wind.

CHAPTER EIGHT

THE CLEAR BRIGHT weather had forsaken them for their journey south. By the time the frowsy revellers were battering in noisy fury at the locked doors of the Hall they were tramping under a grey sky that hung above them like a blanket, the north wind biting at their backs and the first few flakes of the winter's snow drifting down to lie un-melted on their cloaks and furs.

"The weather favours Helge," Ragnar muttered. "If we cannot get the boat across before the inland water freezes then we have failed. And for him, the earlier and harder the frost, the better."

"He will not follow us?" Ness looked back a little anxiously over the bleak land, turning again quickly as the wind seared her face.

Beorn did not lift his head, deep buried in the collar of his sheepskin coat. "He will be certain that we have fled from him in fear. It will please him to think so; he is very proud."

Ness shot a glance at him, but his face was still, so she smiled and let it pass. "If you *had* fled, where would you go?" she asked him curiously.

"I am a Viking. I would not run from anyone," he answered arrogantly, and Ness smiled again. "I would *not* run," he went on, "but if I did, I suppose I would go to my father's kinsman where we will pass tonight. They call him Ole of the Axe, for he will never use a sword. When we return from the Halls of the King I will be a chieftain, too, and ready to be as great as any."

He talked on but before long Ness had stopped listening. Never in her life had she been so cold and, as the day wore on, she could think of nothing but the icy bitterness that gripped her as she struggled on along the open, treeless road. In her soft homeland, where the winter never gripped and the little flowers of spring bloomed frequently at Christmas, they spoke in wonder of a frost that stilled the water for longer than a day. Here the cold was like a living thing, eating through her warm furs to nag her tired body, chilling her afresh with every icy breath she drew. The pretty rime of yesterday was gone and the deadly wind brought the black and wicked frost that froze the lakes and glazed the empty heath.

She remembered little of the homestead of Ole. Not as large as that of Anlaf, there was no big separate Hall for guests, and the house was hospitably crowded. She remembered food and warm ale; the welcome blaze of the fire and the friendly agony of blood returning to her numbed feet and fingers. Vaguely she recalled going with the others to the house of the women. She saw Macha's face above her, and felt the soft, delicious warmth of rugs pulled over her. Gratefully, she slipped down into sleep.

"You will come! Get up, I have something exciting to do. Be quiet, but get up and come quickly!" Above her in the warm darkness, where the firelight wavered on the roof beams, she could see Beorn's face, creased with impatience as he shook her awake.

"Go away! Go away!" Desperately craving for more sleep, she crept deeper into her rugs, but he pulled them from her and dragged her up.

"Wrap yourself well and come with me. We shall have sport!"

Dumbly, thick with drowsiness, she blinked round her at all the others still sleeping warmly. Better go with the wretched boy before he woke them all. Clumsy and slow fingered, she dragged on her warm cloak and hood and followed him out. The dawn was just coming over the eastern rim of the flat land, changing the darkness to iron-grey day. The northern sky still held a pale glow and the listless snow drifted down to lie thinly on the ground.

Beorn was dancing with excitement. "Sport!" he cried. "Ragnar says we may go if we take Arne here with us. We will not start to travel for an hour or so!"

Ness glanced sourly from him to the huntsman who stood beside him, his broad, good-natured face echoing the boy's excitement.

"Whatever it is," she said flatly, "I do not want

to go." She yawned enormously and thought of the warm rugs by the fire, but Beorn shook her by the arm.

"We have found a lynx, girl! Or we have found its trail. There's a pretty fur for you, you can have it for a cap. They are difficult to hunt, very difficult. I have not yet killed one myself. This one was hungry, see, and he crept in to kill among the fowls. I wish I had my dogs with me, but we will go now; you will enjoy it."

Over the light powdering of snow the boy and his unwilling companion could follow easily the soft tracks of the great wild cat which had come in the night to prowl hopelessly round the well protected pens.

"He is gone back to the forest!" cried the boy.

"Let him stay there," growled the shivering Ness.

Deeper and deeper they pushed their way into the forest where the tall fir trees mixed with the spreading beeches, and the experienced eyes of the hunter picked out the tracks of the cat as easily on the soft mossy ground beneath the trees as he had done in the snow.

"He has travelled far," he said doubtfully, "I doubt if we are wise to go too deep into the forest. We will take a long time getting back and my lord Ragnar will not be pleased if we delay the march. I think we should let him go."

But Beorn would not hear of it. "A little more. A little more," he begged. "I cannot let him go now.

See!" He pounced on a small heap of clean-picked bone and damp fur. "See—he has killed! He will rest soon and then we can take him."

So they pressed farther into the heart of the forest until even the determined boy saw wisdom and stood undecided about going farther. "I think," he began regretfully, and then his words were lost in a long melancholy howl that drifted evilly through the forest, followed by another and another—desolate sounds which sent the skin creeping with terror down Ness's spine.

"Let us go back," she whispered hoarsely at once.

Arne stood still and listened, his head turned to the sound. "The howl of a wolf is a good omen going into battle," he said, "but the howl of a hungry pack is another thing when three are alone in the forest. We have been foolish. They are not far off and we must turn at once. There will be another cat." He sniffed the air. "The wind favours us and we have a chance. We will run for it. Now keep together and I will go first."

They raced through the forest, Arne leading them, his keen eyes effortlessly picking their way, the two children behind him hand in hand. Every so often they stopped to listen and there was silence.

"I do not like it," said the huntsman. "A hungry wolf is silent only when he is on the move. We must go faster."

On they raced, weaving in and out between the trees, running, leaping fallen trunks and broken

branches, setting distance between them and the terror of the wolves, making for the open fields in sight
of the homestead, where the wolves would not venture. Always Beorn was a little too fast for Ness, so
that she hardly knew how her flying, tangling feet
kept up with his. Then at the edge of a clearing, he
leapt her over a small pool, flaked with ice around
the edges, slippery with frost. Ness slithered on the
edge as she jumped and fell headlong on the other
side.

"Quick, quick!" cried Beorn. "Get up!" He dragged
at her hand and shouted after the huntsman who was
disappearing into the trees on the other side of the
clearing.

"I can't get up! Oh, Beorn, I can't get up! It's my
ankle!" Ness wailed in fright, struggling to get up
and falling again as the pain shot up her leg.

"It's no good." Fearfully she looked behind her
into the forest and then up at Beorn and Arne, who
had rushed back to them. "You must go on and
leave me."

"Do not be silly," said Beorn, and although Arne
did not speak, his huntsman's eyes were sweeping all
round him, summing up the situation.

"There is nothing to climb," he said in the end.
The tall boles of the firs and beeches rose like pillars. "Besides, they might hold us there for days. We
would be too slow if we carry her. We must make a
fire in the clearing! Quick, Beorn, all the wood you
can gather. Dry wood from underneath the trees."

What is the only thing to
do? build afire,

Beorn and Arne rushed backwards and forwards gathering broken branches, and Ness crawled round as best she could, wincing at the hot pain which seared her leg, scrabbling up the leaves and dead twigs which littered the clearing, lifting up her head anxiously as the long howls drifted again through the trees.

"They are closer," said Arne quietly as he fumbled in his pouch for flint and tinder. "But it is better that they howl," he added to Ness reassuringly. "Now you will be quite all right if you stay close to the fire. I am going for help."

The two children looked at him in dismay, then almost at once Beorn said, "It is wise, Arne. We will be safe beside the fire."

But Ness gazed with wide eyes into the shadows of the dark forest and said nothing, not even turning to look when Arne loped off in the other direction and the first protecting flames crackled scarlet through the smoke above the piled branches.

The wolves were not long in coming. Steadily, stealthily, they came to the edge of the clearing, their eyes glowing green and crimson in the light of the rising flames. There they stayed, almost without moving, only a long head lifting now and again as one of them loosed the evil howl that struck terror into the helpless Ness. Occasionally one more fierce or hungry than the rest moved out from the trees and Beorn would snatch a flaming branch in each hand. Shouting and flailing his fire he rushed at the animal, who would snarl and show its vicious fangs, but would nevertheless lower itself to the ground and slink back among the trees. His voice grew hoarse and the skin on his hands scorched under the smouldering edges of his sheepskin sleeves, but gradually the fire died low and imperceptibly the wolves edged closer.

Ness watched Beorn, looked at him in a quiet moment when boy and wolves faced each other silently across the clearing, a burning branch in each of his hands, the smell of his scorching coat strong on the air. "He is *good*," she thought. "Good and brave, no matter what his silly pride, and I have always known it really. Did not he in the beginning give me back my mother's chain of gold? Now I am his friend and not his thrall and he is willing to care for me with his life. And this is for *me*, not just to protect me from Helge because I am his." A warm wave of affection for the boy swept over her.

"Why do you not *go!*" she cried. "Go and save yourself. *Run!*"

"Don't be stupid!" yelled Beorn in return. "Get more wood! If you cannot walk, crawl, but *get more wood*."

Frantically backwards and forwards she crawled, pain tearing at her ankle on the rough ground, but it was obvious that for all her anguished efforts, the fire was dying. It seemed the animals knew this and waited with a new patience for the flames to sink that they might move in and claim their own. A few were even lying down, long heads along their paws, watching unblinkingly, and in the tired mind of the boy there came a strange confusion that they were no more than his own great wolfhounds from his home and there was nothing he should fear.

He shook his head violently. "More wood, more wood." His voice was hoarse and tired. He dare not take his eyes from the wolves. "More wood, Ness— it *cannot* be much longer!"

Ness did her best, torn with pain and weariness from the effort it cost her to move at all. But in spite of all her struggles the fire burned low, devouring the wood faster than she could gather it. The flames dimmed and fell and from the trees the watching animals moved a little closer.

Beorn shouted and gesticulated. "More *wood!* More wood!" he shouted, but Ness was finished. She edged slowly to the dying fire with her last bundle and threw it in the embers. The sparks which flew up mixed with the cloud of sparks that already danced and flickered against the growing darkness in her head, and the pain in her ankle swirled up and drowned her utterly. Faintly, far away, she seemed to hear a clamour and a shouting, but having thrown her sticks she drooped and fell, her head in the warm ashes and the fur shrivelling on her hood.

She knew nothing of it when, a few seconds later, Arne and the Vikings of Ole burst shouting from the trees.

Ragnar was furious. "One hour I gave you to hunt your cat," he snapped, "not to delay us on the road.

And you waste a day and almost your life into the bargain. Is it not time you learnt sense? By the time we have cared for your hands and the girl's ankle the day is gone. One day could thicken the ice against our passing. You must be mad!"

Beorn could do nothing but look down in flushed shame at his feet, scuffing his toes on the frosty ground, and the huntsman moved to his defence, trying to take the blame.

"You be quiet!" Ragnar turned on him. "You are only to blame in so far as they were children in your care; but you have not the boy's position, and he is old enough to be responsible. Go now," he added to Beorn, "and get Macha to dress your hands, and well or ill we travel at tomorrow's dawn."

Dawn showed Ness's ankle still stiff with pain and twice its size, but there was no time to wait for it to heal. She made the rest of the journey on the back of one or other of the tall Vikings, looking from her perch over the flat unending land that was sinking fast into the deep grip of winter.

This was the Warrior's Road they travelled; the road which held for ever in its stones and grasses the echo of the clash of arms and the sound of marching feet. It was the road that knew the steady step of Vikings marching to the south, avid for new worlds to plunder; knew the slower step of the same armies turning homewards, laden with their booty, and knew also the hasty and disordered footsteps of defeat. On this road in a few weeks' time, Helge would march in all his strength to seek the throne of Denmark.

On this journey, Ness saw no one but the wayfarers of peace. Farmers travelled with their cattle, odd foot travellers went their way in long grey woollen cloaks, and the wealthier, wrapped in fur and sheepskin, rode pale sturdy horses. She saw the occasional band of robbers, who drew prudently away on sight of the company of armed men.

Over the desolate moors the road ran south, often nothing more than a track across the deadly bogs where the grass grew rank and the ice glittered round the edges of the pools. There the greening stones among the sedgy grass were all that held the traveller to a safe path. Through the deep forest the road lay sunk between high banks and the men walked with their hunting spears held ready under the arching trees. Past wide lakes it ran, where pine trees fringed the sandy shore and the water lay grey as steel under the lowering, snow-filled sky. Several times they forded small streams, splashing from frozen bank to frozen bank through the icy water, and, once, where wind-torn thorns leaned above a small river, they saw rising in the distance a mighty mound of fresh earth above the grave of some new-buried Viking.

They avoided such little towns as lay beside the road, for talk would fly quickly of such a company on the march, and they passed the nights as best they could, begging shelter from lonely farmers in their barns and byres. In the far south where the tall stone marked the northern limits of the Roman Kingdom, they passed the night as the unwilling and uneasy guests of a wealthy chieftain who had met them on the road. Ragnar knew nothing of him, and was at great pains to keep secret the purpose of their journey.

The cold and desolation of the last flat stretch of road made Ness's heart ache for her blue mountains and the soft green winter days of Ireland. But it was the end of her journey. The long desolate track, fringed with pines and wind-bent birches, brought them to the river where the longship lay waiting, her captain anxiously watching the ice that fringed the banks and crusted even the middle of the slow-flowing water in the mornings.

Now it was a race between them and the ice. On the river, they kept the boat moving without too much trouble, the gentle flow of the water through the flat land being still sufficient to slow the thickening of the ice. Then the river grew too narrow for the great span of the oars, and they tied ropes to the sides of the longship, teams of Vikings pulling her on either bank, labouring to bring her through the thin sheet of ice which smashed crackling at her bows, loosing the dark water to glitter coldly in the grey daylight.

All the men were needed at the head of the river, one behind the other to place their shoulders under the immense keel, lurching the boat from side to side as they lifted her off the ground. There was no

Viking to spare now to carry Ness so they had placed
her on the deck and, as the boat rose and swayed,
she rolled helpless to the side against the strakes,
scrabbling and squealing and rubbing her bruised el-
bows as she righted herself and peered over the side
at Beorn who held his sides with laughter.

"I like your boats as little on the land as I do at
sea!" she shouted.

"Be quiet!" roared Ragnar, who still looked sourly
on the children. "Be quiet! And keep still, you spoil
the balance with your rolling about!"

Ness was outraged, for who had rolled her over
before she could stop herself? But she was wise
enough to be silent and Beorn turned away to hide
his grinning face.

The waterways were deeper frozen than the river,
and movement difficult and tedious, some of the Vikings pulling the ropes along the banks and others
hanging over the bows, hacking with their axes at the
thickening ice and forcing a passage by inches for the
slow-moving boat. Along the banks, the women and
the children stamped and fretted, weary and unoccu-
pied. Huddled like sheep with their backs to the bitter wind, they watched with anxiety the ice ahead,
fearful that it would prove too thick to pass and that
they would be trapped between the anger of Helge
and the anger of the icy winter in a strange place
where they had neither friends nor shelter.

But they defeated the ice, manhandling the great
ship down at last upon the windswept sands on the

other side of the neck of land. They saw as they launched her that even the edges of the sea were frozen now; patches of the ice had formed that would soon bind together and make a smooth road for Helge to follow where they were going.

It was not until this race with the ice was over that Ness had a chance to talk properly to Beorn. She had not been close to him since the day in the forest and she ached to speak of it.

She had talked a great deal about it to Macha, who shared her pleasure to see signs of gentle-heartedness in the wayward and uncaring boy.

"We pray for him, do we not, Macha? Maybe our prayers are being answered, maybe he has listened to what I have been telling him of gentleness and the teaching of our Lord. Although," her face puckered, "even when he does listen, he usually laughs."

Macha paused in her work, her hands quiet a moment and her narrow grey eyes resting amused and gentle on the girl's face. "You care now, I think, that he should listen? A while ago, he was nothing but a hateful Viking boy and it was no use to tell him anything."

A slow flush crept up Ness's cheeks, and her fingers plucked at the fur around her face. "I don't know. I only know he was good to me in the forest. And brave. So he cannot be quite wicked. Only too proud and rather silly. And it would please you well, Macha," she added shrewdly, "if I could get him to listen long enough to know our Faith. But," her eyes were thoughtful, "I could never *make* Beorn do any-thing. Something would have to happen to bring him to us of his own accord."

He came to her one day where she sat in the well deck of the longship, huddled out of the wind with Macha, preparing the meal of bread and salt fish for the Vikings who rowed steadily for Seeland against the biting northern wind. She spoke to him warmly as he sat down, giving him a hunk of bread which he pressed hungrily into his mouth.

"I have had no chance to thank you," she said, sitting back on her heels, her eyes shining with her new-found affection. "No chance to thank you for what you did in the forest. You saved my life and you could easily have lost yours. You were very brave and good to me. Why did you do it? Why did you not run yourself?"

Eagerly she gazed at him, waiting for an answer, and the boy gazed back, blue eyes wide and dark in his paler winter face.

Then he shrugged and dropped his eyes to his still bandaged hands. "Are you not mine?" he said indifferently. "Must I not care for what is mine?"

Ness leapt to her feet in a blaze of anger, all her affection and kind intentions forgotten; forgotten, too, her injured ankle, which sent her sprawling across the deck. Furiously she shook off Macha's helping hand and scrambled up. She hobbled over and leant on the side of the boat and the winter sea blurred and shifted before the tears of rage and pain which filled her eyes.

She had moved too fast to see the grin of pure mischief which had crossed the boy's face, or the impish wink which he had exchanged with Macha.

CHAPTER NINE

THE HALLS OF the King were similar to those of Anlaf, but infinitely larger and more magnificent. They were heavily defended by great earthworks, themselves protected by water channelled in from the sea. Inside the earthen walls, long rows of cross-beamed barrack halls held the force of the King's warriors, and inside yet another circle of defence lay the living halls of the King himself; vast, carved and gilded and richly furnished.

The longship sailed cautiously up the narrow sound, a long shield hoisted to its mast with the point upwards, to show it came in peace. The voyage had been hard. The sail of the ship hung in tatters and ice caked the carved head at the prow, but Beorn and his friends did not get quickly into shelter. Guards crowded round them, hostile and suspicious of their Jutland speech, plying them with questions as to why and whence they came.

Beorn would have answered arrogantly and thrust them from his way, but Ragnar held him back. He spoke more gently, pleading news of great urgency for the King himself and promising all their arms and loyalty to his service. Still doubtful, the guards agreed in the end to take them to the King's advisers and they were led across the dykes and through the immense wooden gates which breached the earthworks. Ness watched them close behind her, sealed with huge iron bolts, and wondered doubtfully if she would ever see the outside world again. But Beorn bounced impatiently on the balls of his feet and his blue eyes flashed interest and excitement in this new world. Ness moved close to him and, when Macha and the others were ordered to the women's quarters, she passed unnoticed in her shapeless furs and followed the boy and Ragnar round the vast, roughly paved court between the outer and inner walls.

"I will take you to my lord Leif," said the man who had brought them in. "He will know what to do with you. I will take you to the guest hall as you say the boy is the son of a chief." He looked disparagingly at the grimy boy, tired and stained with travel in bitter weather, the burnt patches still black and bare on the front of his sheepskin coat.

But Beorn flung up his head. "Then you will do it quickly, my good fellow. We have travelled long and are tired and have no need to speak with you."

The man looked startled and moved much more quickly to lift the door of a small guest hall, where the fire burnt brightly on the hearth and the cushions along the benches were rich and thick. Gratefully they moved to the heat, easing off their heavy cloaks and feeling the fire draw tingling life back to their faces after the bitter numbing of the wind at sea. Ness stretched out her toes to the blaze and leant back happily against the soft bolsters, blinking in the warmth like a drowsy cat.

Her content was short lived. Suddenly her scalp began to prickle with an uneasy sense of being watched by hostile eyes, and she sat up and peered through the shadows towards the door. They had not heard it open, but inside it now there stood a man so tall that Ness gasped with disbelief even as she nudged Ragnar to attract his attention. The giant saw himself noticed and moved into the room, towering towards the roof beams. He was magnificent in size but, as he reached the fire, the light revealed a deep and horrible scar that grooved the whole side of his face right down into his beard, cleaving the empty socket of his right eye.

"I bid you welcome," he said in a voice of startling gentleness. "I am he whom they call Leif the Giant, and I bid you doubly welcome for they tell me that the boy here is the son of Anlaf. I have known him. Who does not talk of him when tales of bravery go round the table with the ale? He was beside me in my young days when the Frankish axe cleaved my head and had he not fallen above me and dragged me from the field, I would not be here to welcome you today."

He clapped his hands and called for the servants in his strange hoarse voice. He told them to bring food and mulled ale to warm them all after their bitter journey. Then he sat down beside Ragnar, folding his long legs under him and asking for their story, to which he listened carefully, stroking his brown beard. "Helge the Fair," he said at last slowly. "I know nothing of him. Do we need to fear him? What strength has he? What power other than to try and seize the inheritance of a child?"

Ragnar ran his hands through his hair. "I think, my lord Leif, we must fear him. He is young and foolish, but he is very brave and strong and a reckless fighter. He is handsome and daring and men follow him. He has worked long, I think, before my master Anlaf died, to cultivate a following. He lost many of them when we lost the fleet, but there are many more. Now he is joined by his kinsmen in Scania, who threaten the King at the same time from there. He is young, strong, and ruthless—yes, I think we must fear him."

"And the King is old, old, old." Leif the Giant stretched his immense legs out to the fire and Ness on his unscarred side saw his eye wide and brooding on the flames. "He has been a good King. He also has been brave and strong and, for a time at least, made Denmark one country. He has ruled well and for this we respect him still. But he is old—*old*. At times the flame of his wisdom still burns bright, but mostly all fire is dead in his veins. He can no longer lead his warriors into battle, indeed they hardly ever see him, and they are no longer certain for whom they fight. He is only a memory of past glories. To fight well, men must be led by one who can do better than themselves. And now their King cannot do that."

There was a moment of silence. Then the boy asked the question from which the older and wiser Ragnar held back.

"Well, who then, my lord Leif, will lead them into battle against my cousin?"

Leif the Giant looked at him as if in a moment of surprise. "Why, boy? I will. Who else?"

Although he had been perfectly affable in all he said, speaking slowly in his odd soft voice, Ness felt again the shiver of fear that had touched her when she turned her head to see his great bulk inside the door. She fingered the Cross at her neck, and breathed a prayer against evil.

"I do not trust him," she said, when he had left them to their meal, promising that as soon as possible he would arrange for them to see the King.

Beorn and Ragnar both looked at her. "Why not?" they asked together, and Beorn went on, "He seems most friendly, and it warms me to think he knew my father. It is only reasonable that now the King is so old he should have someone younger and stronger to do for him the things he can no longer do himself. Do you not think so, Ragnar?"

"Yes," Ragnar agreed more slowly. "The King at his age must need help. Also I do not see what good it would do the Giant to do us ill. We have no claim except for Beorn's inheritance, when Helge is defeated. What harm is there in that? We have only come to warn of danger and add our small assistance. And yet," his voice was hesitant, "there is something in that voice and those over-fair words that leaves me uneasy."

"M—mm-m." Ness picked happily at the sweet leg of a goose. She wiped the warm juice from her chin and slid her eyes mockingly round to Beorn. "Yes, if I were you I would get out all your charms and half a herd of cattle and start sacrificing to all your muddle of gods at once, for something tells me you will need their help."

Beorn kicked her. "It would do more good than your soft prayers, at any rate. But I am content to take my lord Leif as he is."

As Leif had said, the King was very old. When they first saw him, the children thought it impossible that anyone could be so old, and yet alive. He was very tall, but so bent with age that he crouched in his high chair, down over the arms where his hands rested like yellow talons. Under the sparse wisps of snow-white hair which straggled from his embroidered cap, his face was seamed and shrunken over fleshless bones. But the eyes which looked from this mummy's face were bright and clear and when he spoke, although his voice was high and frail, it was still firm with authority.

"Helge the Fair," he echoed as Leif had done. "It seems to me I knew his father long ago. He was wild, and brave beyond all others. His son may be foolish and ambitious, but he will not lack skill in war. We must be ready for him, though I am troubled over the need to divide our army since he attacks from two directions. But we shall talk of that later in the council. Tell me now of yourself, Beorn Anlafsson, and of your brave father and the manner of his death. I knew him well when I was young and he still younger. He helped me to my throne. Surely he sits now at the Table of the Gods and, shortly, I will join him there if Odin thinks me worthy."

For a moment the old man's eyes clouded and his face grew vague. It was as though, at his great age, simply to speak of it was enough to start him on his long dark journey to Valhalla. Soon he recalled himself and went on talking to Beorn, for whom he seemed to find a special warmth. Hanging in the background lest she be put out if she were noticed, Ness stared all round her at the glories of the Hall of the King. Rich embroideries hung upon the walls. No straw lay on the floor, but shining rugs and soft skins. The chairs and stools and the twin pillars of the gods were richly carved and painted, there was the gleam of silver from horns and plates and the wink of enamel and precious stones from hilt and scabbard. All the wealth and booty of a long life of warfare in far lands was gathered round this ancient in his old age, warm shining proof of past victories.

There were many councils of war as the days went by. Although even Ragnar now accepted the presence of Ness wherever Beorn might be, she was able to

who didn't trust Lief?
— Ness, Ragnar.

find no excuse for creeping after him into these but could only beg him afterwards to tell her what went on.

"We plan," he said a little irritably. "The King's host is to be levied from all the country and then divided into two, one half to face Scania and one to face the middle island from where Helge himself will come. This division gives much concern if Helge's host is large. But there is time to prepare. The ice is barely formed here across the sound and Helge must wait for both the Great and Little Belts to freeze hard enough to bear his army. The Little Belt of water between Jutland and the middle island is always the last to freeze, so we shall be ready when he comes. I wish," his lower lip was thrust out, and he spoke resentfully, "I were old enough to lead even my own small force against him. The Giant treats me as a child and laughs at me. He is quiet and civil, but I know he laughs at me because I am so young."

"The King does not laugh at you," Ness pointed out idly, thinking to please him.

To her amazement, the boy drew himself up and the old arrogant look came over his face. "No," he agreed. "The King does not laugh at me. He keeps me beside him always and takes heed of what I say. My lord Leif must have a care not to treat too lightly one whom the King favours."

Ness gaped at him, but answered as peaceably as she could. "It is no more than the whim of the very old," she said wisely. "And you will do well not to set too much store by it and anger my lord Leif. He is the real power here, I think, and remember you *are* only a child." She looked at him in real distress, alarmed to see his pride running so far beyond reason.

He did not answer but glared at her and stamped away over the fresh snow covering the court. He turned into the forge where he forgot his anger, standing in the warm scarlet glow to watch the rising pile of weapons being hammered out to meet the needs of the growing army of men who were mustering to the call of their King.

The days of waiting were spent in training this ever increasing army, and in the strenuous sports of the Vikings. . . . As Helge had been supreme in all these in the homestead of Anlaf, so Leif was the leader in the Halls of the King. Despite his solitary eye, his javelin flew unerring to the target from first one hand then the other. As the weather closed and the snow grew deeper, the men tied snowshoes on their feet and raced each other long distances over the flat white country under the skeleton trees. Always it was Leif the Giant who reached home first. Always it was Leif who won the wrestling and who excelled in the ball games in the swept court.

Beorn looked on and could not accept it any more than he had been able to accept it from Helge. In all these sports he had not yet the strength to challenge men. He could only watch in jealous gloom and comfort himself with the open favour of the ancient King, who kept him close about him, doting on him and loading him with gifts and favours and unsettling even further the vain, ambitious boy.

"You are stupid," Ness told him flatly. "Your time will come. You cannot be a man while you are still a boy and you must wait. You will be a great Viking yet; don't you defeat the other boys in all these things? But it is not yet your time. You must have patience."

"I cannot wait! I have no patience! I want to be the greatest and strongest of them all. I would have men look at me as they look at Leif and Helge. I want to lead them into battle, knowing that in all feats of arms I shall be the best!"

The girl looked at him. His blue eyes blazed and his dark face shone with the excitement of his dreams. He could well be the greatest of them yet, she thought. He was not tall, but like all the Danes who were of short stature, he was heavy in the shoulders, strong like a young bull. In all his movements he was neat and quick as light, and his head stood proudly on his wide shoulders. Already boys long past his age were unable to defeat him in any of these Viking sports and among them all he was the acknowledged leader. But he could not wait to be a man.

Ness sighed. Almost against her will she had grown fond of this proud and wilful boy, having learnt the kindness that he hid so fiercely under his arrogance, hid it as though it shamed him. But she feared for

What did Beorn want to be—the best man in battle.

him, waiting for the trouble into which his pride and obstinacy would surely lead him. She watched it leading him to folly a few days later.

The weather was clear and fair, with a sky of cold pale winter blue arching over a world which all colour had left. There was nothing but the endless white of snow, sparkling in fringes along the stark blackness of trees and buildings and patching the slate grey waters of the sound with white wherever the ice grew thick enough to hold it.

Out of the bitter cold, the men were wrestling in one of the vast barrack halls, and my lord Leif had joined them. He won as usual and took easily the shouts of praise that followed him as he went to leave the hall. He paused near the door to wipe the sweat from his body and his ravaged face, and to draw on his sheepskin coat against the cold outside.

"My lord Leif." Beorn moved out of the shadows and stood in front of him. "My lord Leif, do you swim?"

The man took the towel from his face and looked at the boy. Ness looked at him too, sharply, for his voice was high and strained and she felt sure he was doing something foolish. She tugged at his arm but he shook her off, and now Leif smiled, his crooked smile, pulled sideways by his scar.

"Of course I swim, Beorn Anlafsson, what Viking does not? But the water now grows dangerously cold unless it be necessary."

Beorn drew himself up, but Ness could see his

mouth was nervous. "Then, my lord Leif, you are tired today after your wrestling, but tomorrow I challenge you to race me in the water across the sound."

The big man stared down at him, searching his face as if to try and understand what lay behind his words. He did not answer.

"It is a challenge, my lord Leif." Beorn's voice was higher still.

At last Leif spoke. "Very well," he said easily in his soft voice, "if it is a challenge I accept it. Tomorrow." He said no more, but drew on his coat and went out past the boy into the bright cold day.

"It is *madness!*" cried Ness. "The sound is already

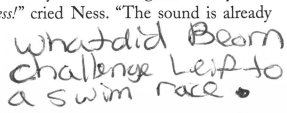

frozen. I have been told men die in these waters, even as they fall in. Your pride is madness!"

Beorn looked at her for a moment as though he would anger. Then, like Leif, he spoke easily and lightly. "The ice is very thin yet. The sound is sheltered and we can break it and clear it easily. As to the cold, it is early yet in the winter and we will move fast. But it will be a trial."

"But *why?*" Ness took him by the arm and stared into the wide blue eyes. "*Why?* What should it matter to you what a grown man can do or cannot do? You defeat all the boys, is that not enough?"

"No!" Beorn's eyes left hers and stared above her head. "Swimming is the only thing in which his strength may not help. I don't know why I must challenge him, but I must. I must be best at *something*. I am a good swimmer. Do you think I shall win?"

Ness shrugged. "If you do, then I think you make an enemy of the Giant. And I do not trust him already. If you think that wise, go ahead."

"Of what account is his enmity?" Beorn answered mulishly. "I have the King's favour."

"The King will not live for ever. Or even for very long," snapped Ness. She gave up the attempt to talk him into sense, and went away to search for Ragnar, to see if he might succeed where she had failed, and then even for Macha, who could often do most with the obstinate boy who regarded her almost as his mother.

Not even she could persuade him from his foolishness. She could only bid Ness say a prayer for him and go herself on the following day to the spot where he should come out of the water—if he did. Here she waited with hot stones, and furs to wrap him and hot stimulating drinks warming on a brazier. The Vikings gathered to watch. They were more silent than was usual when they came to see a sporting challenge; there was none of the usual shouting and arguing and laying on of bets. The hum of talk was low and the men looked puzzled. The challenge itself was unwise at this time of year and it seemed madness at any time for this strange young boy to match himself against their matchless leader.

Even the old King had got wind of what was to happen and insisted on coming to see the race himself. He stood a shapeless bundle of furs beside a brazier on the icy windswept shore, leaning heavily on two companions. His pallid ancient face was untouched with colour by the cold wind which whipped all other cheeks to scarlet. Wilful as the boy himself in his old age, he would not allow that the challenge was foolish and praised Beorn ceaselessly in his thin old voice, calling on everyone to witness his bravery and promising him prizes of great value if he should win.

Ness watched with a heart as cold as the air that nipped her face. She saw no good could come of this; death, maybe, to one or both of them. If Leif should die, who knew what his devoted men would do to

Beorn, in spite of the frail protection of the King? If Leif should win, Beorn's jealousy might well run wild, with the old King to back him up. And if Beorn should win—Ness shuddered that his own conceit would not let him see the danger of an enemy as powerful as the great scarred giant.

There was no stopping now. They threw aside their cloaks and stood one instant waiting for the signal at the water's edge; together they struck the water in the dark channel that had been cleared across the pale ice.

Beorn swam at once. Blinded, stunned, wrenched empty of thought and feeling by the icy shock of the water, the dark depths of his mind still told him he must swim, and he struck out instantly. Leif was older. The shock of the ice-cold water was greater and for a few precious seconds he floundered helplessly. Those seconds were all Beorn needed and Leif never caught him up, despite the long flailing strokes that pulled his huge body through the water like an arrow.

At the other side, Beorn stumbled from the water to fall into Macha's rugs. He gasped for breath, gulping down the hot drink they put to his stiff lips only that he might find his voice to whisper hoarsely, "I did it. I am the *best*."

Leif was pulled out by his friends, far gone, and he saw nothing of the boy's open triumph or the praises heaped on him by the doting King. The watching Vikings looked on in silence, even Beorn's own followers, and Ragnar shook his grey head sadly. Ness walked away and would not look.

Leif the Giant came in the evening to the guest hall. Beorn watched him half fearfully as he came through the shadows to the fire, ready to exchange anger for anger. The Giant congratulated him evenly on his victory and mocked at his own great age which had been his undoing. He praised the boy so generously that Beorn's triumph faded and he was more resentful than ever because, having won, he could not understand why he felt cheated.

The firelight flickered on the lean scarred face, so smooth and expressionless. Ness, waiting outside the firelight with a bowl of broth, watched it and listened to the soft reasonable voice. Despite all the fair words, she felt this man more dangerous than ever for this defeat and knew that Beorn would come yet to suffer at his hands.

Q. Why would Beorn's men and Ness not even watch him — he was showing pride.

CHAPTER TEN

THERE WAS STRAIN between Beorn and Ness after this since she answered only with anger when he showed his foolish pride in the defeat of Leif. She avoided him, keeping with Macha and the other women. She mixed closely for the first time with the other girls, braiding the long red hair they so deeply envied. She learnt the square complex patterns of their embroidery and taught them in turn the softer patterns of her own country. They picked at the Cross at her neck, marvelled at the fine carving in the gold and showed her the small iron hammers of Thor which they wore in the same way. Ness answered all their questions and told them about her Cross and all it stood for. Some were curious and asked more and she told them of her faith as she had told Beorn, remembering all Brother Feredach had told her of the grace of gaining souls for God.

But even as she talked she felt her talking empty. Although she told herself fiercely that he was a fool not worth bothering about, her heart ached for the evenings at the kitchen fire back in the Halls of

What good came from Ness and Beorn being separate.

142

Anlaf and for the boy who had slapped his knees and cried with laughter when she told him of her God. Sadly, she helped Macha with the spinning and the weaving and the cooking and all the other household work, so passing the time she had spent previously as Beorn's shadow.

Great blood sacrifices were offered daily in the temple and Ness and Macha blessed themselves and stared with horror when they were told that some of them were human. The cause was a great one. Animals were not enough. Everywhere the camp seethed with preparations for the coming battles. It was some weeks past the feast of Yul and the winter deep over the frozen land, when the first messenger arrived with news of Helge. The forces of his friends were massing clearly in sight on the coast of Scania where the sound was narrowest. The army of Helge himself was still held on the Jutland coast, waiting for the freezing of the Little Belt.

The old King fretted and worried over his divided army, for the scouts reported the force of Helge's kinsmen as a large one. Leif looked grave. There was yet time while Helge waited for the thickening of the ice, and as the snow-shoed Vikings marched to their positions on the two coasts, Leif still held his councils of war in the Halls of the King.

He pulled his brown beard as was his way when thinking and tapped his charts in front of him on the table. "I am concerned," he said. "Helge has what amounts to two separate armies. Ours is a

force divided and cannot be so well organized, but
I do not see anything else that we can do."

"My lord Leif," cried one of the council, "it is not
like you to sit and wait while the enemy comes to
your door. Why do you not attack first? The ice
across the sound to Scania is hard and thick. Why
do we wait?"

Leif looked at him. "I had thought of that, Eric.
And I do not doubt that your sword of the two
tongues would be in the van of the charge. But we
are heavily outnumbered. A smaller army can do mir-
acles in defence, but I think that to attack would be
to throw ourselves for spitting on the Scanian swords.
Then they could march to Seeland on our corpses."
He smiled. "I would not care for this, rather let
them come and spit themselves on *our* swords when
they are wearied by a difficult march across the ice."

Beorn hovered always on the edge of these con-
ferences, listening eagerly to all that went on, long-
ing to take part. As Leif stopped speaking he moved
up closer to the table where they sat, and spoke with
hesitation unlike his usual self-confidence. "My lord
Leif," he said, "may I speak?"

For one moment a spasm of irritation flickered
across the Giant's face, then he smoothed out his
scarred mask and spoke with his customary quietness. "You are the son of Anlaf. Your cousin threatens to take your inheritance by force, that gives you
the right to speak if you have reason."

At the top of the table the old King's hands were

shaking, beckoning the boy to come beside him. "Yes, yes! Let him speak," he quavered, his head thrust out on its long neck. "Let him speak. Come, son of Anlaf, and stand by me that I may hear you well. Say what you will."

Round the long table, boredom and annoyance lay plain on the Vikings' faces. This was no time for the Ancient One to indulge his whims and they were surprised that Leif allowed it. They stirred restlessly on their stools and exchanged irritable glances as the boy stood up beside the chair of the King and began to speak, his eyes on Leif. As he went on speaking, slowly and carefully explaining his idea, the bearded heads came up and faces lightened; now they exchanged looks of surprise and amusement and even excitement and at the end there were a few shouts of delighted laughter.

Leif's crooked smile creased his long face. "I wonder," he said thoughtfully, and his hand crept to his beard. "I wonder. There is a risk, since if it fails we have nearly all our army on one front, and your cousin could simply march untroubled across the land."

"But it would at least delay Helge's army, and by then a greater force facing Scania would undoubtedly have won a victory and they could turn to meet Helge."

"True, true. It seems too easy." Leif chuckled again. "It would, as you say, delay them. We can try it out down on the sound for it is thick frozen now. We can assume, I think, that Helge will march his army across the beaten track of all the traffic across the Belt. He would not want to plough them through unbroken snow; yes, it might work. It might work indeed. It should be a pretty sight!"

He threw back his head this time and laughed outright, and the deep rumble echoed all round the table. Leif turned to Beorn and spoke more warmly than the boy had ever heard him. "You do well, son of Anlaf— cleverness is often more use in war than thoughtless bravery. You do well!"

He clapped him on the shoulder and, on his other side, the King was plucking at his sleeve with shaking fingers, his head waggling with curiosity. "Tell me what it is at once, I say. I do not understand—I must. Tell me."

Patiently, clearly, Beorn explained again his plan for disposing of Helge's army without losing a man. The old man listened intently, his trembling hand beside his ear, his dimming eyes screwed with the effort of understanding. When the boy finished, he scrambled awkwardly to his feet, fumbling the skirts of his long gown. He placed his yellow hands on Beorn's shoulder and hung above him like a gaunt, stooping bird. "Leif speaks truly." His thin voice wavered with emotion. "You do well, Beorn Anlafsson, and it may be that this plan of yours will save my kingdom. Well, here I promise you before the members of my council that if your plan succeeds I will make you my heir. I have no child, and the throne

you save shall be yours on my death." He bent to
embrace the boy, and the easy tears of old age filled
his excited eyes.

A dead silence fell around the table. Gone was
the excitement and hilarity which had first greeted
the boy's plan and the warmth had left Leif's face.
Even through his own shock, Beorn could feel the
Vikings stiffening on their stools. Nothing was said,
and no man looked at another; all eyes were rigid on
the charts and battle plans which strewed the table.
Even when the boy looked over to Ragnar for encouragement, he did not look up and his face was
weary.

He threw his doubts aside. The King was the
King and his word was law no matter how these
men might feel. He threw back his shoulders.

"I shall do my best, my King," he cried proudly,
"to be worthy of this honour."

The old man subsided shaking in his chair, and
Leif stood up abruptly. "If you have done with us,
my King," he said smoothly as if nothing had oc-
curred, "I think we would do well to try out this
idea of the boy's down on the sound. It should prove
useful."

As one man the Vikings rose and left, making no
sound but the clatter of their wooden stools. Beorn
stared after them and his mouth grew tight. He paid
no heed to the pluckings at his tunic and the husky
praises of the old man who still sat beside him at
the top of the table.

When he saw Ness and told her what had happened, she did not believe him. She laughed out loud. "You? King of Denmark? Why should you? You must have heard him wrongly; sometimes with his piping voice I find him hard to understand."

The boy was furious. "And why not me? Why should I not be a King? I am as good as Helge, yet no one laughs that he should try for the throne! I tell you it is true!"

When he insisted that it was true and told her to ask Ragnar if she needed further proof, she grew angry and exasperated. "And did you not refuse? Is there no limit to your folly? What did my lord Leif say?"

"Nothing." Beorn's face was white with anger.

"Exactly! And how long do you hope to live after the Old One dies? Think you that my lord Leif will take you by the hand and lead you to the throne he has guarded so long? For whom do you think he has been guarding it? You are a fool!"

"That may be!" His blue eyes blazed at her, dark and furious. "But look well where you are and where I am now. I listened long enough to your talk of humility and your God of gentleness. He cares, you say, for those who serve Him! How has He cared for you? He has allowed you to lose your home and your family," he went on cruelly, ignoring her hurt face, shouting at her. "You are nothing now! You are my slave! And I—I am heir to the throne of Denmark! That is how my gods have cared for me!" He chucked at her Cross, tugging derisively at the frail gold chain. Ness snatched it from him.

"Take that thing off, and get yourself a Thor's hammer instead, and see how you fare then!"

Ness was now as wild with anger as himself.

"You will see!" she shouted at him, and her fingers closed firmly on the Cross within her hand. "You will see! You have not yet walked all your road!" For one moment she fumbled for words, trying to tell him of her deadly certainty that Leif meant nothing but evil. Then she gave it up. He would not listen anyway. "You have still a long way to go," she went on. "Later we shall see how your gods have cared for you. Then you may come humbly to mine for shelter!"

The boy snorted. "So! So, let it be! But you forget that it was I who took you for a slave. It is not yet too late to put the iron collar of a thrall about your neck and turn you to the kitchens. You will remember who I am and speak to me only as you should, or it may happen yet!"

Ness glared after him as he stamped away. She ran her two exasperated hands through her hair and then forgot her age and her dignity as the daughter of a chief. Stamping with rage, she stuck out after him all she could stretch of a warm pink tongue. Macha, coming on her, scolded her roundly for her bad manners, but stood beside her to shake her head also after the boy.

When they tried it on the sound, Beorn's idea was a success. On the still, ice-cold air below the

lowering clouds, shouts of laughter echoed across the
ice as the Vikings planned what should happen to
Helge and his warriors. Beorn was everywhere, brilliant in a new scarlet cloak given to him by the
King. He was brimming with pride and delight that
his plan was to be used and basking in all the praise
he got for it. Only if by chance he met Ness did his
face cloud up and his pleasure vanish and she would
always look the other way.

The greater part of the King's army was now
marched back across the island until almost his en-
tire force was mustered facing the enemy on the
coast of Scania.

"Remember," Leif the Giant told them, "it is easier
to fight on land than on ice. Let them come to you.
Do not go after them unless they flee and would
cheat your swords. Use your bowmen and let them
come to you."

He gazed with satisfaction along the ranks of well-
clad, well-armed warriors, fingering their weapons,
wild and fierce at the prospect of a battle. It was
good. All would be well here. He smiled his twisted
smile—life had been too soft under the ageing king.
These men needed a taste of blood.

He let his mind turn to the other very small company which he had put in the charge of Ragnar. They
now faced Helge across the wider sea of ice of the
Great Belt. He had seen to it that they also had a
good company of bowmen, but their most important
weapons were the long iron saws and sharp axes used

by woodmen. Several of the King's foresters were with them. With them also was the wilful son of Anlaf, even though he knew that if the plan failed it meant certain death. Leif shrugged. He had no duty to the child—quite the contrary.

Foot travellers and sledges had made a wide clear track across the ice at its narrowest part, and it was beside this track that Helge had his camp. It was vital to Beorn's plan that he should cross here, and their relief was great when a scout came in breathless from the dark snowy wastes of the sea.

"I have found out that my lord Helge plans to move at dawn on the day after tomorrow. He had thought to find a large host waiting for him and that he might need to cross elsewhere and land up or down the coast. Now he laughs until his fair hair shakes at what his scouts tell him of our tiny company. He feels he is already safe in the King's halls and combs his hair and plaits his beard to look a fine King. He will come straight across the track, he says, and eat this little company to break his fast before marching on through Seeland."

Beorn leapt with delight, and Ragnar's sober face lightened. "He does exactly as we wish him to. Let us see that our saws are sharp as they may be, because we must work quickly and with little light."

As soon as it was dark the next evening, the woodcutters were out on the track across the ice, working by the light of small lamps placed beside them. Well out to sea they sawed great crosses in the ice across

What is the pkin?

the track, cutting deep until they felt the water. This would weaken the ice but not break it. Moving carefully backwards towards the shore until they were in comfortable arrow length, they sawed the ice in big squares, loose floating platforms that would tip the moment weight came on to them. They chuckled as they worked, even as the Vikings had laughed when they tried it on the sound.

"But why, my lord, the crosses cut behind? I do not think anyone will go through there."

"Not at first, not at first. But do you not see—as soon as the leaders step upon these platforms they will tip and sink. The instinct of those following will be to move backwards. Those behind will not know anything is wrong and they will continue to press forwards; this will be too much for the weakened cross-cut ice and down they will all go. We want a column marching firmly, and, if I read my lord Helge's self-confidence aright, he is going to do exactly what we wish him to."

All the rest of the long northern night they waited, sharpening their weapons and burnishing their mail, watching the distant points of flickering light that showed Helge's camp, and looking gratefully upwards as light snow drifted from the dark sky. It was exactly what they needed to cover their tracks on the ice.

"The lights grow nearer!" whispered Beorn hoarsely as the first faint change of colour crept over the night. He was sick with excitement and pride, feeling for the first time the stiff comfort of chain mail worn to protect him in a battle; rejoicing in the heavy safety of the iron helmet that pressed over his eyes. This was the day he had lived for. This was no boy's play but the reality that could bring him death or the glory he so dearly wanted. Ragnar eyed him uneasily, watching his flushed face and brilliant eyes, but he had too much on his mind to do more than hope that when the morning came he would hold to his sense and remember all he had been taught. His bravery he did not doubt.

The scarlet staining of the winter dawn crept up the sky above the snowy land behind them, and as the first blue daylight sharpened on the frozen sea they saw the shadowy mass of Helge's host, pinpointed by the flickering lights of high-held torches.

"They come," breathed the boy, and he felt his head grow light with the rapture of facing his first enemy. "Ragnar, they come."

In utter stillness the eyes of Ragnar and all the Vikings were fixed on the oncoming host. Through the silence of the dawn, far across the ice, they could hear the strange eerie hissing of a thousand snowshoes as the light strengthened and the dark shapes cleared into a spearhead of marching men.

"He will have his beserkers leading," said Ragnar, "the most violent of them all at the front. That will suit us well. They fight like demons, but they have little sense when anything goes wrong."

Beorn tightened his grasp on his bow, his eyes brilliant in the morning cold. "There is not too wide a

column either, there won't be many on safe ground."
He could not hold back a high, unsteady laugh.

"There is not long now," answered Ragnar almost
in a whisper, his eyes unmoving.

The ice glowed blue and white and green under
the risen sun, stretching flat and limitless on either
side of the column that crawled across it like a great
dark animal. They could see the berserkers at the
head, clearly now, huge men in shaggy sheepskins,
hair and beards lifting in the morning wind and
the low sun glinting in their burnished shields. Steadily their great cross-gartered legs pressed across the
beaten path, bringing them closer and closer to the
little force on the shore who watched in such sus-
pense that when Ragnar spoke his voice had failed
him. "They are at the points of weakness now," he
whispered.

Still they came on steadily.

"It has failed!" cried Beorn in high-pitched anguish, and Ragnar laid a steadying hand on his arm.

With comic suddenness the first platform tipped
beneath the leading men. Within an instant they
vanished into the dark water that slopped around
the edges of the rocking ice, and those who charged
forward hoping for safety were caught by the next
loose square. Their wild battle cries changed to roars
of confusion as more and more men were pressed
forward on to the tipping platforms, fighting, if they
kept their feet, to claw their way back again to what
they thought was safety. The front of the column

pressed fiercely back, and, as Beorn and Ragnar had foreseen, the ones behind saw no danger and pressed on. The massive weight was too great for the weakened ice; the cross cuts splintered out in all directions and yelling Vikings slid helpless into the icy water, dragged down by the immense weight of their armour and weapons.

Now it was the turn of the bowmen that Leif had picked so carefully. Ragnar had divided them into three, and two arms spread out on either side of the disordered enemy while the third part approached them from the shore. From all sides they rained a hail of arrows down on the threshing, shouting mass of men who floundered in the breaking ice, breaking more ice and drowning with every moment of struggle. The end of the column, still on firm footing, rallied and fought back but, leaderless and demoralized by the dark jagged chasm ahead filled with their struggling and drowning comrades, they had small heart.

Beorn, wild with success, thought he saw the long fair hair of Helge in the middle of the press and raised his bow, but in the heaving mass of bodies he could not guess what he hit. The enemy crowded together, disaster in front of them, the deadly hail of arrows at their sides. There was not room to raise their weapons or their shields and many of them flung away their arms to make themselves lighter if the ice gave way beneath them. The only way they could move safely was back the way they had come, and this they did, first slowly, then as fast as they could run, chased by the relentless arrows of the King's warriors who came after them. Soon the retreat became a rout and the brave Vikings of Helge fled back across the frozen sea, defeated by a small handful of bowmen and an ingenious boy; leaving more than half their number vanished until the melted ice of spring would bring them forth. Many more lay huddled heaps of sheepskin, their blood spreading wide and pink across the ice.

Long before the victorious warriors were back at the King's Halls they were met by a messenger post haste from Leif. All had gone well with him also. Though the Vikings from Scania were mighty fighters, after a great battle they had been defeated and the host of Helge's kinsmen pursued to the very shores of their own country.

"This is good news." Ragnar put his arm round the shoulders of the exhilarated and weary boy. "Your father would have been proud of you today. Now, with Helge defeated or even dead, you can go home and claim what is yours in peace. The King and my lord Leif will be very grateful and they will surely help you."

Beorn stopped in his tracks and turned to look at him, his uplifted young face glowing in the snowy dusk. "My lord Ragnar," he said slowly and formally, "I think you have forgotten something."

Ragnar's eyebrows lifted and the boy went on. "You forget that this morning I kept my side of a promise made with Denmark's king. Should he keep his side, then I am now his heir."

The older man closed his eyes as though suddenly very tired. When he opened them, he moved as if to speak, but then fell silent. After a long moment he shrugged slightly and slid onwards again across the snow.

CHAPTER ELEVEN

RAGNAR MAY HAVE preferred to forget the old King's promise to the boy, but the King himself had not forgotten.

Leif's army was the first to return, driving their reluctant captives before them at the sword's point. They were drunk with the fierce joy of victory and ready for the thanks of their grateful ruler, whose kingdom they had held from invasion and whose throne they had saved.

He barely gave them a thought. The weary and triumphant Leif came to him as the fire blazed bright against the darkening windows of the Hall and the shouts and yells of the victorious warriors rang round it in the frosty dusk. As he came before his King, his face was bright in spite of his tired limbs and his one eye gleamed with satisfaction.

"You are safe, my King," he said. "They tell me that the boy's plan succeeded on the western shore and all is well. We will not be troubled again for some time by Helge the Fair. If indeed he is still alive. They tell me the drowning and the slaughter were terrible. And your warriors under me fought well and bravely. They look to hear from you."

With the King's great age and frailty, it could not be expected that he would go out himself to speak to the Vikings in the bitter weather. But Leif waited expectantly for the message of gratitude which he could carry to them from the old man whom many of them had served all their lives.

Eyvind the Ancient merely beat on the carved arms of his chair and his bright, restless eyes searched the shadows behind Leif's back. "Where is the boy?" cried the thin voice anxiously.

"The boy?" For a moment the Giant looked blank. "Oh—the boy Beorn Anlafsson? He was with the company on the west coast, they are not yet returned. Only the messenger with news of victory."

"Well then, find out! Find out! Did I not say before you all that if this boy succeeded with his plan, then he would be my heir. Well, he has succeeded and you give him no more thought than if he were the least of our thralls!"

Leif's face had lost its eagerness and showed now only the great weariness of the battle and the long march home. "I do your bidding, my King," he said evenly. "But what of the warriors? Have you no word for them?"

The King waved a fleshless hand. "They did well. But go and find out about the boy!" His voice rose almost to a screech and Leif turned and left him without further protest.

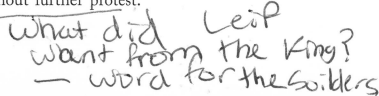

What did Leif want from the King?
— word for the soldiers

He did his best to soothe the angry feelings of the Vikings, who milled around their barracks discussing this latest antic of their Ancient One. Many had crowded into the Hall behind Leif, and in spite of his efforts to make light of it, the whole host of the King's Halls was soon humming with the news that the old man had made the boy from Jutland his heir. Most were wild with anger and indignation, resentful that a stranger should be thrust on them for their next King, and bitter for the slighting of their victory. They still forgave him much because of his great age.

When they had rested and eaten, talking hard around their fires as they swallowed the good hot food, Leif summoned his fighting men again. He crowded them all into one barrack hall, gathering them even on the roof beams that he might speak to them alone, the doors shut against all comers. Respecting him as they did, they listened to him patiently, and although they shrugged and muttered, they agreed in one mighty shout to do the secret thing he asked of them.

So it was that when Beorn arrived in the snow-bright noon of the following day, there was no outcry against him. Even though, in leading in the fighting men, he took pride of place in front of Ragnar. He was received in doubt and silence even more marked than when he had defeated Leif at swimming, but no man's hand and no man's voice were raised against him.

In the weeks that followed he took his place as the King's heir in all the celebrations that followed the victory. In the crowded feasts in the Hall, he sat in the second seat of honour dressed in the finest clothes the old King could give him. He looked down in pride and indifference on those who had supported the Ancient One for more years than he had lived. In the offerings in the temple, he stood at the right hand of the obstinate ancient who insisted still on conducting all the sacrifices himself, even though his trembling and unsure old hands made them a disaster of suffering and spilt blood. Beorn's pride in his place was so great that he could not even spare a moment in his heart to thank for his good fortune these gods of his whose giant statues stood around the temple.

He was completely sufficient unto himself, living in a golden dream of pride and lapped round with the adoration of a foolish old man; and he knew no doubts or fears.

"I thought," he said one day to Ragnar, "that these people might be angry because their Ancient One has declared me to follow him. I am, after all, a stranger, yet I have heard no one speak against me. My lord Leif, who has most reason to be angry since he was the old man's favourite before I came, treats me with greatest courtesy."

Ragnar looked at him long in silence, wondering what words might pierce his pride and confidence, but he could find none. "Your mother," he said at last with a sigh, as though it explained everything, "was as lovely as the spring itself. But a vain and silly woman, unworthy of my great lord Anlaf. There are times you bring her much to my mind."

The boy looked mystified a moment and then a hot flush of anger crept up his cheeks. "I do not understand you. But you grow offensive. Perhaps I rise too high to please even you, my lord Ragnar. Maybe you grow too old to follow me."

As he swaggered away down the room, Ragnar looked after him with a wry grin.

"Yes, my boy. I grow too old for you. Yet if I added on my life again, I would still be younger than the witless ancient on whose every word you hang. Ah well, it takes a wise young horse to know the height of a strange fence." But he shook his head sadly, and resolved to go carefully and not say anything else that might anger the boy, lest in his foolishness he send him away at a time when he never needed him more. Older and wiser than Ness, Ragnar nevertheless shared her sense of foreboding about Leif and had never trusted his soft voice and courteous words.

Ness hardly saw Beorn at all. He made it clear that friendship with a slave was far below his new station, and now when he spoke there was no mischief in his eyes and no wink behind her back to Macha. She saw him only in the distance as he crossed the court or when she went with Macha to wait on the tables in the Hall.

"It is as well I do not see him!" she would mutter angrily as he swaggered past. "He is so foolish that I would only anger him and get an iron collar clapped around my neck to be a thrall!" Then looking after him, her eyes would soften at the memory of the day he had saved her from the wolves, and of the many moments of real, warm friendship they had begun to share before he got this new conceit. Thinking of these things, she would close her fingers on her Cross and breathe a prayer for him.

Once across the crowded Hall he caught her eyes, sad and steady, fixed on him as he talked with noisy arrogance to some high-born visitors. Something in her gaze halted him and his talking died. Doubt and hesitation crossed his face as his eyes looked into hers. He looked all round him for a brief moment as though surprised at where he found himself. Then the moment passed and irritation took the place of doubt. He shook his head angrily at Ness and turned back to his guests. Ness sighed and moved away, and never found him looking her way again.

The dark winter passed and the snow grew thin upon the fields and the ice cracked and crumbled on the deep-blue sound. In the wet fields, the small flowers followed the melting snow and when the farmers walked behind their ploughs the seagulls hung in noisy clouds above them and starred the fresh brown earth with white. Over the whole awakening country blew the warm, wet winds of spring and, for the first time in months, Ness knew again tears of bitter loneliness for the young birch leaves fluttering above her Irish lake and the soft incomparable blue of the mountains of her home.

The land outside threw off its winter shroud and stretched itself in the soft airs of spring, and around the living halls the courts were quick with the voices of children. But inside the great brown ramparts of the King, the old man could not keep pace with the quick surge of the season and daily loosed a little of the grip he held on his feeble life.

He would admit to no illness, and held his councils and presided in his Hall, but his long frame was now no more than yellow skin stretched upon a skeleton, and on his hollow face lay the waiting look of death. On the first warm evening of the blossoming spring, the doors of the Hall had been thrown open to the air. He rose suddenly in the middle of the meal and those around him thought him still too hot and moved to take his cloak. But he turned his head away sharply and his eyes grew wide on the pale spring sky beyond the door. His bent old body jerked itself to its full height, and he made as if to speak. Then his great length crashed like a felled tree. He was not so fortunate as Anlaf. For him, there was no time to call for his weapons or to die in his command. For him there was the Viking shame of death unarmed. His cap off, his sparse white hair disordered, he sprawled to die among the scattered food and upturned bowls, his face downwards towards Hel.

With a fierce shout, Leif stilled the hubbub that rose all through the Hall and laid his hand on the old man's temple.

"He is dead," he said in a moment, and to those who would have spoken, he lifted a hand. He ignored the ones who scurried from the Hall to be the first to spread the news, and turned to Beorn, who stood wide-eyed beside the fallen King.

"Now," Leif said to him, and although he did not raise his quiet voice, it could be heard through all the listening Hall, "you will go. You will go from Denmark and you will stay gone."

Ness, watching from her distance, almost laughed,

How did the King die? — Prideful.

even though she recognized this as the desperate moment that would bring to reality all she had feared from Leif the Giant. Beorn's shattered face and open, wordless mouth were comic in their complete dismay.

"Go?" he managed to say at last, his tongue licking round his dry lips. "I think, my lord Leif, that you forget . . ."

"I forget nothing. And you will go." Leif faced him over the sprawled body, spilt wine creeping through the trailing white hair. "*Nothing*. Did you think for one moment, boy, in your conceit, that I would let you walk in here and take this throne that I have guarded and waited for more years than you have lived? Did you?"

Beorn could only stare at him. Leif laid a hand on the shoulder of the dead man and his face was full of a weary contempt. "I loved him, you stupid child, as I would love a father. He took a doting fancy to you and I would not see him made unhappy by your death. It was obvious that his life was nearly over, so I told my warriors to accept you in peace and make no protest. They could afford to wait with me."

He paused a moment and looked down from his great height at Beorn, almost as white and still now as the dead King himself.

"Were you anybody else," he went on, "I would kill you as a chicken for the pot. But I do not forget the friendship I had with your father, or that he fought above me once to save my life. If you can set

why didn't He Kill Beorn father

aside conceit and learn some sense, you will be just as great as he. Because of him, I give you your life. I give you the boat you came in and the people you brought with you—and I bid you go."

"But where?" The boy looked all round him vaguely and spoke in bewilderment. "Can I not go home to my father's Halls? My cousin Helge being dead, there is none to hinder me?"

"Well, I will not hinder you. I do not care where you go, as long as it is not in the lands of Denmark and as long as you go within the hour. After that I take my sword to those of your people whom I find."

The boy was completely stunned by the speed of his fall from high places. He could not collect himself to think, but looked from one to the other and then back helplessly at Leif. The Giant stared back unmoving. Ragnar moved out and took Beorn by the hand. He led him silent and unprotesting down the steps from the high seats and through the crowded Hall where the Vikings watched in open pleasure. They would have laughed and jibed aloud were it not for the tall figure that stood silent between the pillars of the gods, his hand still lying on the shoulder of their dead King.

Through the door at the back, Ness rushed to tell Macha what had happened, and to help collect together all the Vikings from Jutland and their families. Many of them were angry and resentful, bitter at seeing themselves exiled from their country for the empty ambitions of a silly boy. But they had no choice and little time. As it was the spring, the long-ship was ready and in good repair, out on the water since the breaking of the ice, and they swiftly gathered into her such supplies as they might collect within the hour. Sullen and resentful, they prepared for sea.

"Bear with him," Ragnar begged them. "We are still his people and he is still the son of Anlaf. He has lost all for the moment by his folly, but his day is yet to come. Remember, I say, that he is the son of Anlaf, and bear with him. He has need of friends."

They muttered and grumbled and they turned their eyes away from the boy who came alone aboard the longship in his scarlet cloak, speaking to no one. But they did not speak against him, or turn to offer their allegiance to the Giant and, well before the hour was up, the longship was creeping towards the entrance to the sound. Its carved dragon head was black against the evening sky and a trail of silver flew from its oars in the last of the light.

On board, the little company stared at each other in doubt and shock, facing the open sea and no known landfall.

"Where do we go?" they all asked each other. All except Beorn, who did not speak at all.

"My lord Ragnar," Ness interrupted diffidently after hours of talk. No one had any real suggestion except for the hazardous one of sailing where the wind might take them and throwing themselves on the doubtful mercy of the inhabitants wherever they might land. Within sailing distance of the northern lands, there was small welcome for the Vikings.

"My lord Ragnar," Ness spoke again and, for all her quiet speech, she trembled all over with excitement at the idea she was going to put forward. "My lord Ragnar—could we not go back to Ireland?"

The words came at last in a rush and breathless she waited for an answer. They all turned to peer at her in the cold, starry darkness.

"To *Ireland!*" echoed Ragnar.

"Yes." Now the words came pouring out of her; words she had been preparing since the moment she had stood in the shadows of the Hall and listened to Leif telling the shattered boy to go from Denmark. She grasped her Cross to give her courage. "If you could take me, my lord Ragnar, to the mouth of the river outside the lake that was my home, then I could lead you to my uncle's fort a little farther down the coast. He is a King, only a little King," she added with a side glance at the silent Beorn. "I feel sure that if I bring you as my friends, he will make you welcome. He can always use good warriors."

Ragnar looked interested, but before he could answer the others shouted out against it. "No!" they cried. "No, it would be certain death!"

"We would be attacked anywhere, but *there* where we have killed her people! They would demand our blood! It is a trap!"

"It is not a trap!" Ness shouted but they would not listen.

"*No,*" they said.

"No."

"Madness!"

She turned despairingly to Ragnar.

"I would tell my uncle," she cried, "that in your goodness to me, you have washed out the guilt of killing my family. As a captured slave my life had no value on it, but you valued it and kept me safe. You could have left me to Helge! You could have left me to my lord Leif! If I forgive you my family's death, then so will my uncle. I *know,* I *know!*"

Even as she insisted, a small nag of fear gripped Ness that this might not be true. Would her fierce, loving uncle even wait long enough for her to tell him all this before he fell upon the Vikings and put them to the sword? He *must* listen; these people here had been good to her and she had no wish to see them die.

Ragnar had listened to her, but he was shouted down before he had a chance to speak.

He shrugged. "You see?" he said when they grew quiet. "Myself, I think it might be the best that we could do, but there are too many against me. We will talk again and I will see what I can do with them."

Ness turned away in bitter disappointment and moved over to where Beorn stood under the great dragon's head on the high foredeck. He had stood there in silence since he came aboard, staring into the darkness and ignoring all who spoke to him. He did not speak to Ness now, nor she to him. She stood there beside him through the rest of the dark hours, her sadness and disappointment almost equal to his own. She was content, at least, that he did not turn and send her away.

When in the early morning he spoke suddenly, it was to tear with violence at his soft and gaily coloured clothes, throwing them wildly in the sea as he dragged them off. The scarlet cloak billowed brilliant for a moment on the dark morning sea, then it, too, darkened and was gone.

"By Thor's great hammer," yelled Beorn, "will somebody not bring me some proper clothes!"

When Macha had seen him dressed again in his own more rough and sober garments which she had treasured hopefully, Ness brought him his morning meal. Silently he took it from her and sat down to eat. She sat beside him.

The food went down badly in great difficult gulps, and soon the boy set it aside with a sudden gesture, laying his head down on his knees to hide the hot shameful tears he could no longer hold back. Ness said nothing. She moved round until she hid him from the others in the boat, and allowed him to weep until his misery was eased.

"You will understand," he said at last, wearily, his boy's face old with shame and wretchedness, "it is not the throne of Denmark that I weep for. That is nothing and not for me. It is my own shame, that I was such a *fool!* My pride made me a village idiot with mouth agape and empty eyes. I was no better. Why did you not *tell* me?"

Laughter gleamed in Ness's green eyes and she looked at him sideways. "I did," she said. Her voice was dry and gladly she saw a faint unwilling smile flicker across his miserable face.

"That is better." She moved now to take his hand with warmth and tenderness and to smile at him. "You know you cannot be proud if you laugh at yourself, that was my father's teaching and he was most wise and strong, even though he was so merry with it. There will be another chance to be another Beorn and I *long* for it to be in my country. Let me tell you."

She crouched beside him in the chilly, brilliant dawn as it spread over the tumbling, springtime sea and eagerly she urged on him the plan that they should sail back to her home, but neither her words nor the sharp growing light brought life or colour to the boy's pale face.

His eyes were empty, fixed on the sea. "What do the others say?" he asked listlessly.

"My lord Ragnar thinks the plan good, the others are afraid my uncle will kill them. I *know* he would not. Beorn," she leaned close and laid a warm hand on his arm, "Beorn, show them now that you are still their leader. That is what they need, someone to tell them what to do. They are afraid. Whatever you have done, you are still the son of Anlaf and should be their chief, in wisdom now and with care for them all. I *know* this is wisdom; I know my uncle, and I know these people would be safe with him. Talk to them Beorn. Lead them."

For a moment his tired eyes turned to hers and she saw a spark of the old brilliant blue begin to kindle, and then it faded and he turned back to the sea. "It would be of no use," he said. "They would not listen. I wonder that they did not throw me overboard."

"They would listen," Ness urged. "I have moved among them and heard what they say of you. They are still your people—one piece of foolishness does not alter that. They will listen and be patient with you; have they travelled so far with you to forsake you now?"

He looked at her and then was silent for a long time. At last he stirred. "Let us talk to Ragnar and see if he agrees."

Something of his old eagerness warmed his voice but, looking at his face, Ness knew that never again would he be the proud and heedless boy who had so maddened her with his arrogance. She sighed and left him to go and find Ragnar.

Later, filled with pity, she watched him face the task of standing up alone before his people. He faced them with a humility so new to him it was a painful burden, but he took dignity from his old pride, even though he knew now that it must take a new shape. His people loved him; they had known him since his birth and had suffered with him in his downfall. As

Ness had foreseen, they took him back warmly into their hearts. After the first few anguished words of apology which fell into a listening silence, they were with him, shouting encouragement and willing to hear him.

They had talked all night as to where they should go and many had come round to thinking of Ireland as their only hope. They were too small a company to have much chance on their own. With Beorn's word added to Ragnar's, they were won over and the decision was taken to set course for Ness's home.

Beorn came back and sat down once more beside Ness on the deck. He was moved by the affection of his people, but Ness could see that there was more he was disturbed about, and something else he wished to say. He picked abstractedly at the splinters in the deck and seemed to find it as hard to speak as when he had faced his silent people some while before.

"What *is* it, Beorn?"

"Ness," he said suddenly, "did you see that?"

"Of course," Ness answered gently. "Did I not tell you they would listen?"

"Not only that. For the first time I have spoken to my people humbly. *Humbly*, Ness, as you have always told me. And never have they been so much my people, never have they looked at me like that before. I have learned many hard lessons in these last hours and it seems to me this is another. Maybe I have been wrong to laugh always at your gentle

God. Pride has led me nowhere, nor have my gods who sustained me in it."

He paused a moment and Ness held her breath. Her heart was surging with wild delight and her fingers crept up and closed around her Cross. It would bring her great grace and the happiness that went with it, to win Beorn's soul for God as Brother Feredach had taught her, but at the moment there was a practical reason for her pleasure. If she could tell her uncle that the chief of these Vikings wished to be a Christian and would try and lead his people in the same way, then their chances of a friendly welcome were much greater.

Beorn spoke again. His head was turned away and he did not look at her. It was very hard for him. "Think you, Ness, that this new Beorn who is to find himself in your country, could find himself a new God there also? I think your God may be more suited to the new Beorn."

Ness's face was shining with content. She took both his hands and made him look at her and for the first time since the dark moment in the King's Hall, Beorn's blue eyes kindled again to their sparkling warmth and a contented smile lay on his face.

"I am sure, sure, sure!" Ness cried. "My uncle will have those who can tell you everything of our Faith far better than I have ever done!" She remembered the moment on the mountain in Iona when Beorn had likened God the Father to a brave Viking as he had sacrificed his own Son. She shook her head and laughed aloud. "But what of your people?" she asked then.

"I cannot speak for them at once. But you know as well as I that Macha already has many of the women to her way of thinking. I have heard them at their prayers. And in these things, I have noticed that where the women lead the men may follow." He grinned his old wicked grin. "I am not sure that that is not what has happened to me."

Ness punched him and then jumped up out of his way. "Let us go and tell Macha."

Macha wept tears of pleasure and she hugged and kissed the embarrassed boy until he fled from her. Then she turned and hugged Ness, both for gladness over Beorn and for pleasure over their return to Ireland.

"Though home in Ireland, I have none," she sighed. "It was all so long ago and I have nothing and no one to go back to. Except," she smiled tenderly, "Ireland."

Ness kissed her. "Do not fret, Macha. There will be a home for all of us with my good uncle, that I am sure of now."

She turned to Beorn who leant pale and weary against the dragon's head, exhausted now that all his ordeals were over, but his eyes were content.

Ness smiled at him. "It is well?" she asked.

"It is well." He threw himself down on the deck in the warm sun. Even as she looked at him, he slept.

CHAPTER TWELVE

SOME DAYS LATER, after a wild northern passage in the spring winds, they were in sight of the blue hills of Ireland which Ness had last seen through her lonely tears. Beorn came up beside her as she stood gazing at them.

"The old hermit," she said suddenly, remembering the last time she had looked at that coast. "You laughed, remember, because, you said, his God could not save him. I said we must not question God's ways. Do you see now, if the old man had not been brought aboard, you would never have begun to think about his God! I think now he died for you—and for all your people who would perhaps follow you into his Faith. I am sure he would think it well worth dying for!"

Beorn did not answer, but stared a long time at the blue shadow of land and then turned away in silence.

As they drove on, Ness did her best to school herself against the sight of her home. When they passed the wide bay where the fishing huts clustered at the mouth of the river leading to her lake, she did her best to look at it without remembering too much. But the faces of her mother and father and her five brothers and sisters rose before her and her agony was as fresh as if she had lost them yesterday. She turned from the loved familiar sweep of blue mountains and shining water and threw herself thankfully into the task of guiding the ship southwards. She watched carefully for the opening in the hills which would take them up the long inlet to her uncle's fort, and consoled herself with the happy thought of his surprise and delight to find one member of the family still alive.

"What if they attack," asked Ragnar, "without waiting to find out who you are? To them, we will look like any other Black Strangers."

"I have thought of that. The fort is some distance from the shore and there is nobody down by the water to attack us. You will anchor in the middle of the water and I shall row ashore with Beorn and Macha only; no one will attack a woman and two children. And once we land," she smiled happily, "there will be plenty of time for them to see us coming and for them to know me. We visited my uncle often for, as you see, it is no distance by water. All his servants know me well."

She stood hopping at the rail of the longship as it nosed its way up the inlet, shouting to Beorn to look at this or that; trying to draw the still pale and quiet boy into the excitement that would not allow her even to stand still. She fell silent only at the last, as they rounded the final bend and saw the fort in the distance, crowning the long gentle slope which led up from the water. Vast trees grew below and round it and the white walls, which circled the green hillside, gleamed softly in the sun.

Now Beorn really looked. He thought of dark, heavy buildings, turf roofed against the winds, low and strong against the bitter winter. "It is so white!" he said in amazement. "And the grass so green. It is beautiful."

"They say," said Macha proudly, "that the High King's white walls at Tara can be seen by a man still two days' journey off across the plain!"

She breathed deeply and her eyes glowed in her gaunt face as she stared hungrily at the green fields and the blue hills she had thought never to see again. It was with difficulty that Ness woke her from her dream and got her moving towards the small boat lowered from the longship.

Ness was right in thinking she would soon be seen and known. With Beorn and Macha, she dragged the skiff on shore, fumbling and scrabbling in her excitement. They set off up the gentle slope of the hill to the fort, but long before they reached the first gates in the lowest palisade a wicket was flung open and her uncle's servants rushed out to greet her. Macha they welcomed also, and gladly, but looked in doubt and hatred on the young Black Stranger until Ness told them sharply he was her friend, and they must show him manners.

"And lead me quickly to my uncle!" she cried, brushing away the questions and ignoring the curious faces that stared back in amazement down the hill to where the Vikings stared in turn from the longship.

Her uncle was waiting for her, striding to meet her down his long painted hall where the bright shields hung above the carved chairs and the four tall candles burnt serenely at the corners of the square fire. He set them dancing in the wind of his passing, as he caught her up and crushed her to his great red beard. He held her off then to listen as she burst into her gabbled story of how she had come beneath his walls in a longship and claimed the Black Strangers for her friends. In a while she realized he was not listening but smiling above her head at something behind her. She was too full of words to stop, however, and rattled on to try and press into a few minutes all the long dark months of her Danish winter.

"Ness!" he said at last, shaking her gently by the arms. "Ness—my little niece, my brother's child—look round."

Something in his voice and look stopped her at once and for a moment she stared up at him, searching his warm loving eyes. Then she turned round.

The wide doors of the Hall were open to the bright spring day, and between her and the light stood a tall woman in a blue gown, her hair the same dark red as Ness's own. Beside her were ranged five children, from the tall fair son down to the staggering baby who clutched the hand of the smallest girl. As Ness turned her arms were already out and, without a sound, the child flew to them. Then she was crying and laughing, clutching, feeling her hair, struggling for belief.

"My mother! My mother! My mother!" was all she could say as the happy tears poured down her radiant face. At last she pulled herself away to be kissed and hugged and almost torn apart by her delighted brothers and sisters.

"But how?" she said at last. "How, how, *how?* They told me I was the only one alive on the island." She hugged the crowing baby to her cheek. "How?"

"Your father always remembered the coming of the Black Strangers in his youth, and long ago he made for us a secret underground chamber in the wood behind the house. When the time came to use it, we could not find you. It was as simple as that. We saw you afterwards—we watched you sail away; but we could do nothing to help."

"My father?" Ness asked next, but without hope.

"He died as he should, my daughter, with the people of his village. But now," she went on quickly, to push away the shadow that fell across them all, "let us hear what became of you, my tall strange daughter. I hardly know you for the little Ness of last year's summer."

Sitting on a bench beside her uncle's blazing hearth, her mother's arm around her and her family gathered close, Ness told her long tale. Her mother listened quietly, smiling and holding out her hand to Macha when the child explained who she was. She looked faintly puzzled over gaps in Ness's story at the time when she was in the Halls of the King and turned a thoughtful eye upon the boy who stood quiet and apart, whose name had not been mentioned.

"I am glad you are back," she said when it was all ended, "for we shall need you. When your brother Cormac is old enough to handle the farm, we will move back to the island. Your uncle thinks me foolish, but the lake is our home. It will be lonely, though, with all the other islands empty and your father gone."

Ness stared at her. "Mother, mother!" She fought to free herself of the tangle of small brothers and sisters all around her. She scrambled to her feet heedless of the candle flame that scorched her sleeve, facing her mother with her green eyes wild with eagerness. "Mother—it need not be so! They need not be empty!" She banged at her sleeve and flapped away the smell of burning wool. "All the Vikings that have come with us are farmers, they are called only to fight as they are needed. Many of them have their families, for like me and Macha they would not be left with Helge. Macha can have care of our home. She will rule us all, and my lord Ragnar grows older and would gladly settle in peace to care for the farm with Cormac. And best of all, the chieftain of these people has told me he will become a Christian and lead his people to do the same. Please, my mother, my uncle, forgive them the blood of our tribe and let them settle here in peace. There would be a home for all those who have been good to me, a place for everyone." She clutched her scorched arm, heedless of pain, her shining eyes pleading from her mother to her uncle. They looked at her and their glances met and agreed.

"It seems," her mother said, "as though after all this time, our misfortunes may turn to help us. Your generosity does you credit, my daughter, and this happy day brings back a lot that we have lost. As you say, these people cared for you when they had no duty to, and it means much to us to hear that their chief will take our Faith. We will forgive them, Ness, and they shall have a home. But," her voice was gentle, "there is one person of whom you have not spoken." Her eyes were on Beorn, who stood silent in the shadows outside the plans and the rejoicing and the excited talk. "What of the boy, Ness? Who is he, and has he no place? And what is he if he is not your friend?"

Ness turned and grew suddenly quiet, looking at the boy. Then she moved over to him, her feet scuffing in the rushes in the silence that had fallen. Without speaking, she put her hand in his and led him back across the Hall to where her mother sat.

"This is Beorn, son of Anlaf. He is the chieftain of these people of whom I told you. It is he who will become a Christian with the help of my uncle's priests. There is much I have not told you as to why we left Denmark in such haste, but these things he would prefer to tell you himself. He is good and he is kind and he is brave, and I owe him my life not once but several times, once when it could easily have cost his own. He is my special and most precious friend, mother, and the best place of all must be for him."

Her mother's eyes had been travelling from one child's face to the other, sensing the depths of something that had happened to them, sensing the loneliness and bewilderment that still lay behind the boy's pale quiet face.

She smiled and took his hand away from Ness. "Well then, he is the chieftain of his people. He has his place with them. But I think he should have a place among us also."

She moved the six children into line again, Ness taking her place now as second in the family. Then she put out a hand and separated Ness from Cormac. Into this space she put Beorn. "There," she said gently, "I think he fits perfectly. There is his place for as long as he wishes."

The boy fell on his knees and tried to kiss her hands. She lifted him up. "I do not expect that from my sons."

She turned to all the people who had crowded affectionately into the smoke-dimmed Hall. "And who knows," she said, "if we settle all together on these islands as Ness plans, there may come a day when the striped sails of the Black Strangers will billow again across our lake. If they find there people of their own kind, speaking their own tongue, then perhaps we can persuade them not to kill and pillage, but to learn instead to be our friends and trade and settle with us."

Ness clapped her hands together and skipped with happiness. "Oh," she cried, "thank God for this happy day!"

Beorn spoke beside her and she turned on him wide-eyed.

His grin broke clear and merry. "Yes," he said, "I said thank God, not thank the gods!"

ABOUT THE AUTHOR

"IT HAS ALWAYS been my idea to try to portray
events in which children become involved in the dra-
matic past. And it is, of course, infinitely more plausi-
ble to create adventures in past centuries, when it was
perfectly possible for them to be abandoned with the
need to look after themselves." Madeleine Polland provided ample proof of her ability to create such adventures—she wrote eighteen children's historical fiction
titles over a period of sixteen years.

The author was born Madeleine Cahill in the
south of Ireland in 1918. She vividly remembers the
fighting and burning during the Irish Rebellion in the
early twenties, before her father moved the family to
England. There in a small town north of London the
three brothers and two sisters spent a happy childhood. Madeleine was great friends with her brothers,
and was an irrepressible tomboy. As she grew older,
her interest in art caused her to prepare for a career
in clothes design. Her plans changed dramatically
when her mother became ill and Madeleine stayed
home and cared for her. She got a job at the local
library, and had the delightful task of rebuilding the

library's book collection. Later, during World War II, she enlisted and served at a radar installation. In 1946 she married Arthur Polland. Their two children provided inspiration for various of her books—they appear (only thinly disguised) in the interesting mystery story, *Stranger in the Hills.*

It was the suggestion of a friend that decided Madeleine to try her hand at writing for children. Her first attempt was *Children of the Red King*, published in 1960. Then came *Beorn the Proud* a year later, followed by many others, including a number written for the *Clarion* series published by Doubleday.

Her books are marked by a desire to portray real people in whatever historical situation they are in. Her characters are more than simple paste-board cutouts amiably showing the reader important moments in history. For most of her novels, she was able to imbue the story with an authentic air by personally visiting the locale of the books—only *Chuiraquimba and the Black Robes* (set in Paraguay) and *Mission to Cathay* (set in China) had to be completely reconstructed from other sources.

Madeleine Polland died in 2005.